# The Luminal Chronicles –
## Aether's Legacy Unveiled

Robbie Dexter

INDIA • SINGAPORE • MALAYSIA

ISBN  979-8-89415-286-8

# CONTENTS

# PROLOGUE

In the realm of Lumaria, where Aether and magic intertwine, two luminaries emerged as beacons of innovation and wisdom. Aetherius Luxarum, the Aetherial Luminary, stood at the helm of the Luminary Consortium, a master of Aether manipulation with principles that illuminated the path to enlightenment. Lumina Solara, the Aetherial Mentor, guided aspiring mages through the intricacies of Aether manipulation, encouraging harmony and creativity in magical practices.

In the hallowed halls of the Luminary Consortium, Aetherius Luxarum addressed the gathered members with words that resonated like echoes of ancient spells:

"Aether, the essence that courses through Lumaria, holds boundless possibilities. In the dance of light and shadow, we find the secrets of its manipulation. Let us embark on a journey to create new forms of magic, unlocking the potential that lies dormant within."

Aetherius Luxarum's principles of illumination, resonance, harmony, aegis, and amplification became the guiding stars for Luminary Consortium members, forging a path toward unity and strength.

Beside him, Lumina Solara, with a staff aglow with Aetherial brilliance, addressed the assembly of eager mages:

"Magic is a symphony of elements, each note contributing to the harmony of Lumaria. Let us delve into the fusion of Aether with elemental forces, infusing spells with newfound power. With attunement and synthesis, we shall carve a legacy of innovation in the annals of magical knowledge."

Under Lumina Solara's tutelage, mages embraced the principles of Fusion, Elemental Infusion, Elemental Attunement, Elemental Harmony, and Aetherial Synthesis, expanding their magical repertoire beyond conventional boundaries.

Together, Aetherius Luxarum and Lumina Solara ignited a spark of creativity within the Luminary Consortium. The call for a new form of magic echoed through the air, promising an era of innovation, unity, and the unraveling of mysteries hidden within the luminal tapestry of Lumaria. The journey had begun, and the Luminary Consortium prepared to chart new territories in the vast expanse of magical possibilities.

In the ancient scrolls of prophetic lore, a celestial *prophecy* unfolds, veiled in mystic symbols and enigmatic verses. The words whisper of a forthcoming epoch, where the fabric of magic shall be woven anew, and the weavers shall be known as the Beati of Magic Creation.

"When stars align in cosmic dance, and Aether's breath embraces every chance,

The Beati shall emerge, their hands ablaze, crafting magic in mysterious ways.

From Lumarian shores to the Atlantean tides, their essence blends, and power abides.

A symphony of elements, a dance of light, creation awakens, transcending night.

*Yet, heed this warning, O seekers of might,*

*For woven threads hold perilous sight.*

*In the forge of creation, shadows may sway,*

*Unraveling secrets that led astray.*

*The Beati's gifts, both boon and bane,*

*A double-edged sword in magic's domain.*

*For every creation, a shadow may brew,*

*A danger concealed, a price to rue.*

In pursuit of wonders, tread with care,

The line 'twixt creation and chaos, beware.

For where Beati weave the fabric of dreams,

Echoes of peril may rupture the seams.


As destiny's loom begins to weave,

The Beati of Magic Creation conceive.

Yet, their fate entwined with shadows dark,

A cosmic dance, a delicate embark.


In the alchemy of chaos, secrets unfold,

A balance sought in the tapestry's hold.

For in the dance of creation and strife,

Lies the key to harmonize Aether's life.


Seekers, beware the lure of power,

In the Beati's hands, both bloom and cower.

For magic's creation, a blessing's grace,

Yet, shadows linger in the sacred space.


Heed the prophecy, its cryptic tone,

The Beati's saga, yet unknown.

In the symphony of cosmic elation,

Unravel the threads of magic creation."

# CHAPTER 1

# SHORES OF DESTINY

In the earliest days of his youth, Kaelin, a wide-eyed and curious seven-year-old, found solace in the embrace of Eldermere's shores. The coastal village, a guardian between the ancient forest and the vast sea, cradled him with the rhythmic cadence of waves. The sea, a constant lullaby, whispered tales of an innate magic that coursed through the very fabric of his being.

**Young Kaelin (7 years old):**

The dense forest that marked the outskirts of the village beckoned to Kaelin, even at his tender age. It was as if the ancient trees themselves recognized the child, their branches forming a protective canopy that seemed to guide him on his explorations. The forest became a playground of discovery, and Kaelin felt a connection to the towering sentinels that watched over him.

One fateful day, with the whispering sea guiding their steps, Kaelin and his childhood friend, Lirael, aged five, embarked on an adventure that would shape their destinies. The moonlit ruins revealed themselves, bathed in an ethereal glow that cast shadows dancing in the moonlight. A hidden waterfall beckoned, concealing a chamber within the ruins—a chamber that held secrets older than time itself.

Entering the heart of the hidden chamber, Kaelin felt a tingling sensation, an energy responding to the innocence and purity of his young spirit. Luminescent symbols adorned the walls, telling tales of a Lumarian civilization lost to the annals of history. Unbeknownst to the young boy, the very magic that defined Eldermere stirred within him, resonating with the ancient energies of the chamber.

His tiny fingers brushed against the weathered pages of an ancient tome. As the pages flickered with images, Kaelin's eyes widened with wonder. The sea, a constant source of fascination, whispered arcane wonders that only a child's heart could comprehend. In this enchanted space, Kaelin felt a surge of magic within himself—unseen threads connecting him to the very elements that surrounded Eldermere.

## Fast forward to Kaelin (Present - 18 years old):

The memory of that childhood discovery lingered as Kaelin, now a young man of eighteen, found himself drawn once again to the forest and the ruins. With Lirael by his side, the ancient stones welcomed them, resonating with the echoes of their youthful exploration.

In the presence of the hidden chamber, Kaelin sensed the familiar tingling sensation, a resonance that connected him to the forgotten magic of Eldermere. Memories of Lumarian symbols pulsating with life flooded back. The realization struck him—enhancement and conjuring magic were at his command, gifts unlocked by the ancient chamber.

Kaelin turned to Lirael, a glint of realization in his eyes. "Lirael, do you remember this place? The chamber, the ancient tome—it feels like a dream, yet here we stand."

## Lirael (Present -16 years Old):

Lirael's eyes widened with recognition, her memories resurfacing. "Yes, Kaelin, I remember. We were just children, and yet, something about this place drew us in. The magic... it feels alive."

## Kaelin (Present):

"The sea guided us then, just as it guides us now. I can feel the magic within me, Lirael. Enhancement, conjuring—I can manipulate the very essence of Eldermere."

Lirael nodded, a shared understanding passing between them. "And the sea? What does it tell you?"

Kaelin closed his eyes, listening to the subtle whispers of the sea. "Water magic. The sea recognizes my affinity for its power. Eldermere's magic courses through me, and I am part of its ancient tapestry."

Together, Kaelin and Lirael stood in the moonlit ruins, the echoes of their childhood mingling with the newfound revelations of their present. The sea, a constant companion, seemed to embrace them in its eternal dance, as the magic of Eldermere unfolded in the hands of these two intertwined souls.

# CHAPTER 2

# WHISPERS OF THE PAST

---

**Flashback - A Childhood Discovery:**

Long before the weight of destiny pressed upon Kaelin's shoulders, a curious boy of seven stood at the cliff's edge, overlooking Eldermere's vast expanse. The sea, a companion since his earliest memories, whispered enchanting secrets only he could understand.

With the innocence of childhood, Kaelin traced Lumarian symbols in the sand, mimicking the dance of waves. His small fingers grazed the ancient stones, a connection forming between the young mage and the magical currents that cradled his village.

Beside him, another child of five, with eyes gleaming in wonder, watched the patterns he drew. Lirael, an inquisitive spirit even at a tender age, had joined Kaelin in his exploration.

Lirael's eyes widened as Kaelin's fingers danced across the Lumarian symbols. She sensed a magic, subtle yet undeniable, in the air. "Kaelin, what are these?" she asked, pointing to the symbols. The sea seemed to respond to her question as if inviting her into the mystical conversation.

**Transition to the Present:**

Back in the present, as Kaelin approached the same ruins, the air shimmered with a nostalgic energy. The memories of his childhood discovery merged seamlessly with the determination of the present. Lumarian runes responded to his touch, recognizing the continuity of his journey.

**Kaelin (Present):**

The echoes of his childhood discovery mingled with the present reality. "This place... it's like a bridge between my past and present," Kaelin murmured to himself. Lumarian runes responded to his touch, their glow intensifying, as if acknowledging the continuum of his journey.

## Lirael (Present):

Lirael, now a trusted companion on this magical journey, observed the Lumarian symbols with a knowing gaze. Memories of their childhood exploration filled her mind, and she felt a sense of shared destiny with Kaelin. "We've come a long way," she remarked, her voice carrying the weight of their intertwined fates.

## Young Lirael's POV:

Lirael's eyes, even at the age of five, bore the spark of a natural explorer. As Kaelin traced Lumarian symbols in the sand, her gaze flitted between the patterns and the dance of the waves. A gentle breeze stirred, carrying with it the salty tang of the sea and the subtle fragrance of the forest.

Curiosity radiated from Lirael as she crouched beside Kaelin, her small hand mimicking his movements in the sand. "Kaelin, what are these?" she asked, her finger pointing to the Lumarian symbols. The sea, as if responding to her innocent query, whispered with a soft melody, a prelude to the elemental revelation about to unfold.

Kaelin, sensing Lirael's curiosity, smiled warmly. "These are Lumarian symbols," he explained, his voice a gentle cadence in sync with the rustle of leaves. "They're like a language that connects us to the magic of Eldermere."

As Kaelin continued to draw the symbols, Lirael's surroundings seemed to respond to her presence. The air around her shimmered with a subtle energy, and she felt an inexplicable connection to the elements. Unbeknownst to both children, Eldermere recognized the nascent magical affinities within them, a symphony of potential waiting to be harmonized.

## Elemental Revelation:

In a playful moment, Kaelin conjured a small orb of water, the liquid shimmering in the moonlight. Lirael's eyes widened in awe as the water orb hovered between their palms. The sea breeze carried a hint of approval as if acknowledging the emergence of a water affinity.

Excitement danced in Lirael's eyes as she extended her hand toward the water orb. To her surprise, a playful zephyr manifested, encircling the water with a gentle breeze. The elemental display unfolded like a hidden dance choreographed by the magic woven into their very beings.

Kaelin, now caught in the delightful revelation, encouraged Lirael to explore further. With a focused gaze, Lirael attempted to manipulate the Lumarian symbols to conjure a small flame. The air responded to her innate connection, and a tiny flame flickered to life at her fingertips.

As the flame danced, a tremor in the earth beneath them marked the emergence of an unexpected affinity. The ground beneath Lirael's feet seemed to pulse in tandem with her excitement, revealing an earth affinity that mirrored the ancient roots of Eldermere.

A Triad of Affinities:

In that moonlit moment, Eldermere witnessed the revelation of Lirael's triple affinity—a harmony of air, fire, and earth. The sea, the air, and the ancient earth whispered their approval, weaving a tale of a young girl destined for a magical journey.

## Young Kaelin's POV:

Kaelin's memories drifted back to the pivotal moment when his magical abilities first manifested. At the tender age of seven, his connection to Eldermere's magic deepened, unveiling the untapped reservoirs within him.

It was during a playful exploration with Lirael that Kaelin discovered his latent enchantment and conjuring abilities. The forest, a realm of mysteries and hidden wonders, became the backdrop for this extraordinary revelation.

## Discovery of Enchantment:

In the heart of the ancient ruins, a place that had become their secret sanctuary, Kaelin and Lirael stumbled upon a forgotten altar adorned with Lumarian symbols. The air within the ruins seemed to hum with anticipation, and Kaelin felt a tingling sensation in his fingertips.

As he touched the Lumarian symbols, a gentle radiance enveloped him. To their amazement, flora around the altar responded, blooming with vibrant colours under Kaelin's unintentional enchantment. Flowers unfolded, and vines intertwined in a dance choreographed by the young mage's newfound ability.

Lirael's eyes widened with wonder as she witnessed the enchantment at play. Kaelin, his own eyes reflecting the surprise and awe, realized that Eldermere had gifted him the ability to breathe life into the very essence of nature.

## Awakening of Conjuring Magic:

Emboldened by the enchantment's discovery, Kaelin's adventurous spirit sought to explore the depths of his magical potential. The ruins resonated with the Lumarian energies, and a hidden chamber revealed itself—a space where the elements converged in a harmonious dance.

With an innocent desire to impress Lirael, Kaelin focused his thoughts on conjuring a small elemental companion. The air shimmered, and a mischievous wisp of wind manifested, swirling around them. Laughter echoed through the ruins as the conjured breeze played with their hair, a testament to Kaelin's burgeoning conjuring magic.

The sea, always a silent guide, murmured its approval. Kaelin and Lirael, their bond strengthened by shared magical revelations, embraced the enchantment and conjuring bestowed upon them by Eldermere.

## Connection to Water Magic:

As they continued their explorations, the sea's whispers became more pronounced. Kaelin, drawn by an invisible thread, approached the water's edge. He extended his hands toward the sea, feeling a surge of energy resonating within him.

To his amazement, the water responded to his command. A small wave rose and danced in rhythm with Kaelin's movements. The sea, recognizing his inherent connection, unveiled the gift of water manipulation—a synergy of magic that mirrored the ebb and flow of Eldermere's tides.

In that moment, the Lumarian symbols etched in Kaelin's memory seemed to glow with a newfound brilliance. The enchantment, conjuring, and water manipulation wove together, forming the cornerstone of Kaelin's magical identity. Eldermere, it appeared, had chosen him as a guardian of its ancient, elemental magic.

Kaelin and Lirael, bathed in the afterglow of their magical discoveries, shared a knowing glance. Little did they realize that these childhood revelations were but the first whispers of a destiny entwined with the very fabric of Eldermere's enchanted existence.

Kaelin and Lirael, unaware of the profound significance of this elemental dance, shared a joyous laughter that echoed through the moonlit glade. The Lumarian symbols, etched in the sand, seemed to glow with a newfound luminescence, mirroring the magical potential that lay dormant within the tranquil village of Eldermere.

## Young Lirael's POV:

Lirael's memories wove a tapestry of enchantment, drawing her back to the golden days of her childhood spent exploring the verdant wonders of Eldermere. With each step down memory lane, she could feel the soft grass beneath her feet, smell the fragrant blossoms that adorned the landscape, and hear the gentle melodies of the forest echoing in her mind.

Amongst the many treasured memories, those shared with Kaelin held a special place in her heart. Together, they embarked on countless adventures, their young minds ablaze with curiosity and wonder. In the embrace of Eldermere's mystical beauty, every discovery felt like unlocking a secret of the universe.

It was during these formative years that they crossed paths with Master Elowen, a luminary whose presence illuminated the very essence of their village. Master Elowen was a figure of wisdom and grace, revered by all who knew his magic. His knowledge of magic seemed boundless, and his teachings opened new horizons for young apprentices like Lirael and Kaelin.

Under Master Elowen's guidance, Lirael and Kaelin delved deeper into the mysteries of Eldermere. They learned the ancient rituals that honoured the land's magic, studied the intricate patterns of luminal pathways, and explored the hidden depths of the enchanted groves.

Master Elowen's lessons went beyond mere incantations and spells; he instilled in them a reverence for the natural world and a deep understanding of the interconnectedness of all things. Through his teachings, Lirael and Kaelin discovered the harmony that existed between the magical and the mundane, and they grew to appreciate the delicate balance that sustained Eldermere's beauty.

As Lirael reminisced about those enchanting days, a sense of gratitude welled up within him. Master Elowen had not only been their teacher but also a guiding light that had shaped their understanding of magic and their place in the world. His influence lingered in every spell they cast and every journey they undertook, a testament to the enduring legacy of her wisdom and compassion.

Though time had passed, and their paths had diverged, Lirael carried the lessons of her childhood with her wherever she went. In the depths of her heart, the memory of Master Elowen remained a source of inspiration and guidance, a beacon of light that illuminated even the darkest of days. And as she ventured forth into the unknown, she knew that her connection to Eldermere and the teachings of her beloved mentor would forever guide her on her magical journey.

# CHAPTER 3

# LUMARIAN MENTOR

In the heart of the Lumarian ruins, Kaelin and Lirael stood before the altar, their eyes reflecting the vibrant hues of newly bloomed flowers under Kaelin's enchantment. The air tingled with magical resonance, and as they revelled in their newfound abilities, a wise presence approached—the luminary figure of Master Elowen.

**Master Elowen POV's:**

Master Elowen stood tall amidst the enchanted glade, his presence commanding respect and admiration. Clad in robes of deep forest green, he exuded an aura of timeless wisdom that seemed to merge seamlessly with the natural world around him. His staff, crafted from the heartwood of ancient trees, bore witness to the countless journeys he had undertaken and the vast knowledge he had accumulated over the years.

As he observed Lirael and Kaelin's magical display with keen interest, a soft glow illuminated his weathered features, casting a warm light upon the scene. The Lumarian runes etched into the altar shimmered in recognition of the children's efforts, resonating with the ancient energies that flowed through Eldermere's very essence.

Approaching the enchanted altar with measured steps, Master Elowen's voice carried the weight of centuries past, echoing with the wisdom of generations long gone. His words were like a soothing melody that reverberated through the glade, instilling a sense of calm and reverence in all who listened.

"Ah, young ones," he began, his tone gentle yet imbued with authority, "you have uncovered the Lumarian legacy that lies dormant within Eldermere's ancient roots. The magic that courses through you is not merely a product of your abilities but a reflection of the profound connection between our village and the primordial forces that shape its destiny."

As he spoke, Master Elowen gestured towards the surrounding landscape, where the vibrant hues of nature danced in harmony with the ethereal energies that permeated the air. It was as if the very land itself responded to his words, acknowledging the sacred bond that existed between the inhabitants of Eldermere and the mystical powers that guarded its secrets.

"You are the guardians of this legacy," he continued, his voice carrying a note of solemnity, "entrusted with the task of preserving its sanctity and passing it on to future generations. May you always remember the lessons of our ancestors and the importance of living in harmony with the natural world?"

With a final nod of approval, Master Elowen turned to leave, his steps guided by the wisdom of ages past. As he disappeared into the depths of the forest, his presence lingered like a gentle breeze, leaving behind a sense of peace and purpose that would forever shape the lives of those who had been touched by his teachings.

## Counsel for the Young Mages:

In the shared memory of Lirael and Kaelin, Master Elowen emerged as a beacon of guidance, his presence weaving through the fabric of their magical awakening like threads of an enchanted tapestry. As they stood before him, bathed in the soft glow of Eldermere's luminal pathways, they felt a sense of reverence and awe at the wisdom he possessed.

Master Elowen's voice, like the gentle murmur of the sea, carried the echoes of ancient knowledge and boundless possibility. As he spoke, the whispers of the sea seemed to intertwine with his words, adding an ethereal quality to his teachings.

"Your connection to Eldermere is profound," Master Elowen continued, his gaze piercing yet filled with warmth as he looked upon the young apprentices. "Every bloom under your enchantment, every wisp of conjured breeze, and the graceful dance of manipulated water—they all bear witness to the Lumarian heritage that flows within your veins."

As he spoke, the very air around them seemed to shimmer with the resonance of their magical potential, as if acknowledging the sacred bond between the children and the land that nurtured them. It was a moment of profound realization for Lirael and Kaelin, as they understood that their magical abilities were not just individual talents but a reflection of their deep connection to Eldermere and its ancient legacy.

With Master Elowen as their guide, they delved deeper into the intricacies of their magical gifts, honing their skills and expanding their understanding of the mystical forces that surrounded them. His teachings were not just about mastering spells and incantations but about embracing the inherent harmony between nature and magic, and the responsibility that came with wielding such power.

And so, under Master Elowen' s tutelage, Lirael and Kaelin embarked on a journey of self-discovery and enlightenment, their hearts filled with gratitude for the luminary figure who had illuminated their path. As they continued to learn and grow, they knew that they carried with them the timeless wisdom of their mentor, guiding them through every challenge and triumph on their magical journey through Eldermere.

## Connection Forged:

## Present time:

In the sacred confines of the Lumarian chamber, a profound bond blossomed between Master Elowen, Kaelin, and Lirael. It transcended mere memories, becoming a pivotal moment that intertwined their destinies. Like threads woven into a tapestry, their connection would shape the future of Eldermere, forging a path filled with shared purpose and unbreakable unity.

As they stood amidst the ancient ruins, bathed in the soft glow of luminal pathways, the echoes of their shared magic reverberated through the chamber, filling the air with a sense of reverence and anticipation. Kaelin, Lirael, and Master Elowen found themselves united in purpose, their individual strengths and abilities intertwining to form a formidable alliance—a trinity of magic destined to safeguard the enchantments of Eldermere and guide its inhabitants toward an extraordinary fate.

Master Elowen, with his boundless wisdom and unwavering resolve, stood as the guiding light, offering his knowledge and guidance to the young apprentices. His presence infused the chamber with a sense of tranquillity and assurance, as if reassuring them that they were on the right path.

Kaelin, fueled by curiosity and a thirst for knowledge, brought his innovative ideas and daring spirit to the table. His innate connection to the magical energies of Eldermere allowed him to see possibilities where others saw limitations, and his determination to push the boundaries of conventional magic ignited a spark of inspiration in his companions.

Lirael, with her keen intuition and deep respect for the natural world, served as the grounding force within the trinity. Her affinity for elemental magic and her ability to commune with the spirits of Eldermere lent a sense of balance to their group dynamic, ensuring that their endeavors remained in harmony with the land they sought to protect.

Together, they stood as guardians of Eldermere's legacy, their bond forged in the crucible of shared experiences and mutual understanding. As they gazed upon the Lumarian ruins, they knew that their journey was just beginning—a journey filled with challenges, triumphs, and the promise of a future illuminated by the boundless magic of Eldermere.

In that Lumarian chamber, amidst the whispers of ancient spirits and the hum of arcane energies, Kaelin, Lirael, and Master Elowen pledged themselves to the noble cause of preserving the enchantments of their homeland. And as they stepped forward into the unknown, they did so with hearts full of determination and a shared sense of purpose, ready to face whatever challenges lay ahead and to forge a future worthy of the magical legacy they had inherited.

# CHAPTER 4

# AETHERIC AWAKENING

As they ventured deeper into the chamber, a hallowed space enveloped in the luminescent glow of ancient runes, the air crackled with arcane energy. Lumarian whispers, carried by the ethereal winds, guided them through the labyrinthine passages, each step echoing with the weight of untold histories. Master Elowen led the way, his connection to the mystical currents of Eldermere serving as their compass in this otherworldly sanctuary.

Kaelin, attuned to the subtle shifts in magic, felt the resonance of Lumarian runes etched on the chamber walls. The symbols pulsed with a gentle radiance, telling a story that transcended time. The Aetheric energies within him stirred, responding to the ancient enchantments that surrounded them. He traced the symbols with his fingers, absorbing the silent teachings embedded in the very fabric of Eldermere.

As they delved deeper, the chamber unveiled hidden alcoves adorned with relics of Lumarian history—crystalline artifacts, ancient tomes, and murals that depicted pivotal moments in the magical lineage. Each revelation carved a path through the labyrinth of their understanding, connecting the present to the echoes of the past.

Lirael, with her affinity for the elements, could sense the harmonious dance of Aetheric energies within the chamber. The very stones seemed to hum with the secrets of long-forgotten spells, and the air shimmered with the remnants of ancient incantations. She moved with a dancer's grace, attuned to the unseen rhythms of the magical currents.

Master Elowen, a guardian of Lumarian knowledge, interpreted the intricate tapestry of magic that adorned the chamber. He explained the significance of each symbol, each relic, weaving a narrative that transcended generations. The chamber, a living archive of Lumarian heritage, responded to his presence, revealing its secrets in response to his inquiries.

The deeper they ventured, the stronger the Aetheric resonance became. Lumarian runes on their skin pulsed with a shared heartbeat, creating a bond that transcended the physical realm. Eldermere, a realm suspended between reality and magic, mirrored their journey inward as well as outward, reflecting the depths of their collective purpose.

In the heart of the chamber, a focal point bathed in an iridescent glow, a mural unfolded—the convergence of destinies, the intertwining threads of each Lumarian's journey. Their silhouettes merged with the vibrant hues of magic, marking a reunion with a destiny that had been intricately woven through the ages. As the Lumarian chamber whispered its secrets and revealed the interconnectedness of their paths, Kaelin, Lirael, and Master Elowen stood united, ready to embrace the unfolding saga that awaited them in the mystical embrace of Eldermere.

The luminescent glow of the Aetheric nexus lingered as Kaelin, Lirael, and Master Elowen emerged from its embrace. The air seemed to shimmer with newfound energies, and the echoes of Lumarian legacies resonated through Eldermere. Yet, the shadows of the past cast subtle veils upon the village as the trio ventured forth.

Kaelin, now attuned to the Lumarian tapestry within Eldermere, felt a profound connection to the magical currents that flowed through the village. The Aetheric convergence had unlocked memories of his father's mastery and his mother's enchantments, creating a bridge between generations.

## Unveiling Shadows:

As they walked through the moonlit paths, a sense of foreboding clung to the air. Eldermere's tranquil facade masked the whispers of shadowy secrets. Kaelin's luminescent eyes scanned the surroundings, seeking the source of the veiled darkness that danced at the periphery of his senses.

Lirael, her triple affinity echoing the Lumarian revelations, noticed the subtle shifts in elemental energies. The air felt charged with an undercurrent of unrest, and the flames in the torches flickered erratically. Her heightened connection to Lumarian magic allowed her to sense disturbances in Eldermere's delicate balance.

The Lumarian Guardian's voice echoed in their minds, a cautionary whisper. "Lumarian legacies unravel not only the light but also the shadows that lurk within. As stewards of Eldermere's magic, you must face both, for the echoes of history bear burdens as well as blessings."

Master Elowen, his form flickering between the ethereal and corporeal, sensed the disturbance. The Lumarian Guardian's warning resonated with his ancient wisdom, and a somber expression crept

In the heart of Eldermere, a secluded grove revealed ancient statues—a memorial to Lumarian mages who had faced the shadows of their legacies. The moonlight cast elongated shadows, and the air felt heavy with the weight of untold tales.

Kaelin approached the statues, his eyes narrowing in recognition. The figures depicted Lumarian mages wrestling with shadowy manifestations of their past. Elyndor Wayan and Avonlea Aquafin, his parents, stood among them, their expressions a testament to the struggles they had endured.

As Kaelin touched the stone surface, whispers of betrayal and forgotten alliances echoed through his mind. The Lumarian Guardian's voice grew more solemn. "The shadows that veil Eldermere carry echoes of a past where trust was shattered. Unravel the threads of secrecy, for the Lumarian legacy demands both revelation and redemption."

Lirael, too, felt the weight of the shadows. Elemental energies whispered of ancient conflicts, where fire clashed with water, air stirred tempests of mistrust, and earth crumbled beneath the weight of hidden truths. The grove seemed to hold the scars of Lumarian struggles.

Guided by the Lumarian Guardian's wisdom and Master Elowen' s steady presence, Kaelin and Lirael delved into Eldermere's shadows. The veils that obscured the village's history began to lift, revealing a tapestry woven with both brilliance and betrayal. Unraveling the past would be the key to safeguarding Eldermere's future.

As the moon reached its zenith, the Lumarian echoes intertwined with shadows set the stage for a journey that would test not only the strength of magic but also the resilience of bonds forged in the crucible of Lumarian legacies.

CHAPTER 5

# WHISPERS OF BETRAYAL - LUMARIAN SHADOWS UNVEILED

The grove, bathed in the moon's silvery glow, became a stage for revelations as Kaelin, Lirael, and Master Elowen grappled with the echoes of Lumarian shadows. The statues stood as silent sentinels, bearing witness to a past steeped in both brilliance and betrayal.

Kaelin's luminescent gaze swept across the statues, each telling a tale of Lumarian mages facing their inner demons. As he traced the carved features of his parents, Elyndor Wayan and Avonlea Aquafin, his heart stirred with a mix of pride and apprehension. Yet, one statue drew his attention—an enigmatic figure caught in the throes of shadowy turmoil.

A realization dawned upon Kaelin. The statue, once obscured by the shadows, now revealed its true identity—Master Elowen, the venerable mage who had guided Kaelin's steps since childhood. The Lumarian Guardian's words echoed in his mind, "Unravel the threads of secrecy."

Lirael, too, sensed the revelation in the air. The grove's ambient magic whispered of Master Elowen's connection to the Lumarian shadows. Her eyes widened in realization as the pieces of the puzzle fell into place, intertwining Eldermere's fate with the choices of a Lumarian mage.

**Master Elowen's Silence:**

Master Elowen, his ancient eyes holding the weight of Lumaria's history, observed the unfolding recognition in his protégés. Lumarian shadows cast long echoes, and the time for concealment had ended. Yet, a subtle sadness lingered in his gaze, a lament for the trials that lay ahead.

Kaelin, compelled by the need for understanding, stepped closer to the statue of Master Elowen. The Lumarian Guardian's voice, tinged with sorrow, resonated within the grove. "Master Elowen, a stalwart luminary of our esteemed consortium, stood unwavering during the tumultuous events that unfolded in the past. His valiant efforts in the face of adversity have woven his story into the very fabric of Lumarian history. The shadows that surrounded him, shrouded in a cloak of discretion, now call upon you to unravel the concealed truths and discover the depth of his Lumarian legacy.

## Kaelin's POV:

"Master Elowen," Kaelin spoke, his voice carrying a mix of curiosity and trepidation. "What shadows haunted you? What Lumarian legacy did you face?" The grove seemed to hold its breath, awaiting the revelations that had been concealed for too long.

The statue, though frozen in stone, emanated a spectral presence. A voice, laden with the weight of Lumaria's secrets, whispered through the grove. "Betrayal and sacrifice, choices that reverberate through time. Lumaria, once a beacon of unity, faced fractures that echoed in the hearts of its mages."

As Master Elowen' s words echoed, visions unfurled before Kaelin's eyes. Lumarian mages, torn between loyalty and diverging paths, faced a pivotal moment of betrayal. The grove transformed into a spectral theatre, where shadows danced with the remnants of bonds sundered by secrets.

Lirael, too, witnessed the Lumarian betrayal through the elemental currents. The air carried the echoes of whispered oaths, the flames flickered in the wake of fractured promises, and the earth beneath the statues seemed to mourn the bonds that crumbled.

Master Elowen, stepping forward, spoke with a tone that resonated with both mentorship and melancholy. "Lumarian legacies bear the weight of choices. The shadows that haunt Eldermere are intertwined with the betrayals of a bygone era. Facing these shadows is the path to redemption."

Kaelin and Lirael, their eyes meeting in silent acknowledgment, felt the gravity of Lumaria's legacy settling upon their shoulders. The Lumarian Guardian's voice, now a solemn oath, surrounded them. "Unravel the shadows, for in redemption lies the key to Eldermere's enduring magic."

As the moon cast its silvery glow, the grove stood as a testament to Lumarian shadows unveiled. The statues, frozen in time, seemed to implore the young mages to confront the echoes of betrayal that lingered within the heart of Eldermere.

# CHAPTER 6

# THE VOID SHAPER'S OMEN

The grove, now haunted by the revelations of Lumarian shadows, became a nexus of contemplation for Kaelin, Lirael, and Master Elowen. As the Lumarian Guardian's words lingered in the air, a subtle disturbance in Eldermere's magic hinted at the encroaching presence of the Void Shaper.

Kaelin, his senses heightened by the Lumarian revelations, felt a disturbance in the magical currents. The grove's tranquillity wavered, replaced by an eerie undercurrent that sent shivers down his spine. His gaze shifted to the horizon, where a shadowy veil seemed to encroach upon Eldermere.

**Whispers of the Void:**

Void Shaper—an enigmatic figure whose existence blurred the boundaries between magic and the void. Eldermere, once a haven of serenity, now resonated with the ominous whispers that heralded the Void Shaper's approach. The Lumarian Guardian's voice echoed in Kaelin's mind, "The shadows are not the only threat Eldermere faces."

Lirael, attuned to the elemental energies, sensed a dissonance in the harmony that Eldermere once held. The air, fire, and earth whispered warnings of a looming darkness. Her eyes mirrored the concern etched on Master Elowen's face as the grove braced for the arrival of the Void Shaper.

Master Elowen, his gaze piercing the shadows that gathered on the outskirts of the grove, spoke with a grave solemnity. "The Void Shaper—a wielder of forbidden arts, a weaver of shadows beyond the known realms. Eldermere's tranquillity is at stake, and we must confront this looming threat."

As the shadows deepened, a figure emerged—a silhouette cloaked in the essence of the void. The Void Shaper, a harbinger of discord, stepped into the moonlit grove with an otherworldly grace. A hushed silence befell the ancient trees as the grove became a stage for the convergence of Lumarian legacies and void-born shadows.

Kaelin's hand instinctively gripped the hilt of his Aetheric blade, a Lumarian legacy that now resonated with a sense of urgency. The Lumarian Guardian's guidance echoed in his mind, urging him to stand firm against the encroaching darkness.

The Void Shaper, his presence an echo of void-born power, spoke with a voice that seemed to ripple through the fabric of reality. "Eldermere, cradle of magic, your serenity wanes. The shadows that dance are but a prelude to the abyss. Lumarian mages, heed my presence, for your legacy teeters on the brink."

Master Elowen, a pillar of resilience in the face of looming shadows, addressed the Void Shaper with a stern gaze. "Your presence defiles the sanctity of Eldermere. Lumarian legacies endure, and we shall not yield to the void's seduction. Speak your purpose, shadow weaver, and face the consequences of trespassing."

As the Void Shaper and the guardians of Eldermere stood in a tense standoff, the grove bore witness to the clash between Lumarian resilience and void-born malevolence. The air, once filled with whispers of Lumarian legacies, now echoed with the ominous tones of an impending confrontation—one that would decide the fate of Eldermere's enduring magic.

The echoes of the Void Shaper's ominous presence lingered in the grove, intertwining with the ancient melodies of Eldermere. Kaelin, Lirael, and Master Elowen stood amidst the towering trees, their gazes reflecting the resolute determination sparked by their Lumarian legacies. Shadows clung to the edges of Eldermere, awaiting an opportune moment to encroach upon the cradle of magic. However, a subtle shift in the air signaled the awakening of Lumarian defenses.

Kaelin, attuned to the Lumarian whispers echoing in his mind, felt his Aetheric blade thrumming with newfound vitality. Each beat echoed the Lumarian Guardian's guidance, encouraging him to delve deeper into the reservoir of potential within. The Lumarian legacy, dormant for too long, stirred within him as a slumbering giant roused from its rest.

Eldermere, the ancient guardian of magic, responded to the imminent threat. Lumarian runes, etched into the very essence of the landscape, began to glow with a flash of ethereal brilliance. The grove itself seemed to exhale a luminescent breath, as if awakening from a timeless slumber. Eldermere's defenses, woven into the fabric of the land, readied themselves to repel the encroaching shadows.

Lirael, her triple affinity resonating with the elemental energies, sensed the response of Eldermere's guardians—the ancient trees. Their roots, like tendrils of magical awareness, extended into the Aetheric nexus beneath the grove. Lumarian and elemental forces intertwined, creating a harmonious dance of magical threads that pulsed with anticipation.

As Kaelin and Lirael stood side by side, their Lumarian legacies intertwined with the Lumarian Guardian's guidance. The grove became a symphony of magic—Aetheric, elemental, and the Lumarian essence blending into a powerful crescendo. Eldermere itself seemed to vibrate with Lumaria's acknowledgment of their determination to face the impending darkness.

Master Elowen, the venerable mage whose existence spanned the annals of time, issued a command that resonated through the very roots of Eldermere. His words were not just a command but a call to the ancient enchantments that lay dormant. "Lumarian defenses, awaken! Shield this cradle of magic from the encroaching void. Let the legacy of Lumaria shine bright, resilient against the shadows that seek to unravel our tapestry."

The grove transformed into a sanctuary of radiant energy—a Lumarian Aegis. Lumarian runes, now aglow with collective strength, coalesced into a luminous barrier. This Aegis surrounded Eldermere, pulsating with the combined might of Aetheric, elemental, and Lumarian forces. The shadows, like tendrils of inky darkness, recoiled as they encountered this impenetrable shield.

Confronted by the formidable Lumarian defenses, the Void Shaper, a creature born of the void's abyss, hissed with frustration. Unable to breach the sanctity of Eldermere's magic, it retreated into the shadows, leaving the grove bathed in the soft glow of the Lumarian Aegis. Eldermere's magic, now reasserted, breathed a sigh of relief.

Kaelin and Lirael, standing within the protective embrace of the Lumarian Aegis, felt a profound connection to the cradle of magic. The grove whispered assurances of resilience and enduring magic, as if Eldermere itself acknowledged their commitment to its safeguarding. The Lumarian Guardian's voice resonated with pride, "Eldermere stands strong, its magic intertwined with Lumarian legacies reborn."

Master Elowen, the sage whose eyes held the reflections of countless ages, observed the triumphant repelling of the void-born threat. Eldermere's magic, resilient and timeless, bore witness to the awakening of Lumarian legacies—a testament to the enduring spirit that safeguarded the cradle of magic.

As the grove settled into tranquillity once more, Kaelin, Lirael, and Master Elowen understood that the shadows had been unveiled but not vanquished. The Lumarian legacy, rekindled by the confrontation, now faced the challenge of navigating the unfolding tapestry where shadows and Lumarian light interwove in an eternal dance.

# CHAPTER 7

# SHADOWS ENTWINED - UNSEEN THREADS

Eldermere's grove, basking in the afterglow of the Lumarian Aegis, retained a newfound serenity. Unbeknownst to Kaelin, Lirael, and Master Elowen, a figure lingered on the outskirts of the magical haven. Aric, a young man with a latent affinity for shadow magic, moved through the borderlands, his existence concealed from the watchful eyes of Eldermere's protectors.

**Aric's POV:**

Aric, a solitary wanderer with an inexplicable connection to the shadows, roamed the periphery of Eldermere. The Lumarian Aegis, softly glowing in the distance, stirred a curiosity within him. Little did Aric know, his every step was observed by a subtle force—a dark influence that sought to exploit his latent potential.

The shadows, sensing Aric's untapped abilities, whispered cryptic promises to him. A seductive murmur that hinted at power, recognition, and the fulfilment of desires. Aric, drawn by the allure of the shadows, ventured deeper into the borderlands, oblivious to the strings of destiny quietly entwining around him.

Unseen by Eldermere's protectors, the Void Shaper seized the opportunity presented by Aric. The young man, a vessel of unexplored potential, became a conduit for shadow magic, manipulated by the Void Shaper's subtle machinations. Threads of shadowy influence extended from the Void Shaper, weaving a web around Aric's unsuspecting form.

As Eldermere's guardians remained focused on their duty, Aric, in the shadows, unwittingly danced to the tune of forces unseen.

Eldermere's grove, bathed in the soft luminescence of the Lumarian Aegis, stood as a sanctuary of tranquillity. Kaelin, Lirael, and Master Elowen, unaware of the clandestine movements on the outskirts, continued their exploration of Eldermere's enchantments. Meanwhile, Aric, a mere silhouette in the borderlands, was about to become entangled in a web of shadowy intrigue.

Aric's footsteps carried him deeper into the borderlands, the whispers of the shadows growing more pronounced. The Lumarian Aegis, like a distant beacon, both fascinated and unnerved him. Shadows clung to him like sentient companions, guiding him to a secluded clearing where an ancient gnarled tree stood.

As Aric approached the ancient tree, the shadows seemed to converge, forming an ephemeral veil around him. The air thickened with an otherworldly presence, and the temperature dropped as if the shadows themselves absorbed the warmth. Aric, entranced by the mysterious energy, felt an unseen force probing the depths of his latent magical affinity.

In the heart of the clearing, a silhouette coalesced from the shadows—a manifestation of the Void Shaper. Dark tendrils extended from this shadowy figure, intertwining with the shadows enveloping Aric. The Void Shaper's voice echoed, its tone resonating with an unnatural harmony that both seduced and commanded.

"Welcome, Aric," the Void Shaper's voice reverberated through the clearing. "You are chosen, a vessel for the shadows. Embrace your destiny, and the power of darkness shall be yours."

Aric, caught between fascination and trepidation, hesitated. The promises of power echoed the desires he harboured in the depths of his heart, yet an unspoken warning tugged at his consciousness. The shadows, both comforting and foreboding, wove around him, leaving an indelible mark on his destiny.

Unbeknownst to Aric, the Void Shaper's influence seeped into his very being. Arcane sigils appeared on his skin, marking the acceptance of a pact written in shadows. The latent affinity for darkness within him surged, and Aric's eyes, once ordinary, now reflected the abyssal depths of the void.

As Eldermere's guardians continued their endeavors within the magical haven, a new player had entered the stage—the unwitting vessel, Aric, ensnared in the shadows' intricate dance.

While the shadows whispered secrets to Aric in the secluded clearing, Kaelin, Lirael, and Master Elowen ventured deeper into Eldermere's heart. The Lumarian Nexus resonated with a vibrant energy, and the trio found themselves standing before an ancient gateway leading to separate chambers—a gateway that concealed trials that would unravel their latent potentials.

Master Elowen, the guardian of Eldermere's magical heritage, spoke with a voice that carried the weight of ages. "Beyond these gates lie trials designed to unveil the depths of your magical affinities. Kaelin, Lirael, embrace the Lumarian Aegis, for within its embrace, your legacies will awaken."

## Kaelin's Trial:

Kaelin, guided by a resolute determination, stepped through the gateway into a chamber pulsating with Aetheric resonance. Lumarian runes adorned the walls, casting a soft glow that danced with his every movement.

As Kaelin stood in the centre, the ambient Aether began to respond to his innate magic. He extended his hands, feeling the currents around him. The Lumarian Guardian's voice echoed, guiding him to delve into the essence of his water-based magic.

## Unlocking Aquamancy:

A surge of energy enveloped Kaelin as he channelled his connection to water with newfound clarity. Drops of water materialized around him, floating in mid-air. As his control intensified, the water formed intricate patterns—a dance choreographed by the synergy of Aether and aquatic magic.

Kaelin marvelled at the spectacle, realizing that this was Aquamancy—a Lumarian legacy awakened within him. The water responded to his every thought, shaping itself into ethereal sculptures. In this Aetheric convergence, Kaelin embraced his aquatic affinity in a way he had never imagined.

The Lumarian Nexus revealed itself in the heart of Eldermere, a crystalline pool surrounded by ancient stones inscribed with arcane symbols. The air vibrated with the convergence of Aetheric energies, and the Lumarian runes on Kaelin's skin pulsed with newfound vigour.

Guided by an unseen force, Kaelin approached the crystalline pool. The whispers of the sea and the ancient forest merged into a unified hum, directing his gaze to the nexus. Memories, not just of Lumarian heritage but of his own journey, echoed within him.

As he peered into the pool, the Aetheric energies unravelled fragments of his father's legacy. He saw Elyndor Wayan, his father, manipulating Aetheric blades with finesse. The visions transcended time, revealing ancient rituals, powerful enchantments, and the forging of connections between Lumarian mages.

Emotions swirled within Kaelin, a mix of awe and trepidation. The Lumarian Guardian's voice resonated within the nexus, addressing him.

"In the Aetheric convergence, you glimpse the legacies woven into Eldermere's fabric. Your journey is entwined with Lumarian history, and each step you take echoes the footsteps of those who came before."

Kaelin extended his hands toward the nexus. A radiant glow emanated from the pool, symbolizing the awakening of Lumarian legacies within him. The Aether, now attuned to his journey, pulsed with anticipation, heralding the next phase of his magical awakening.

The Lumarian Guardian's voice lingered in his mind, guiding him through the Luminal secret art of Aether Magic. The water around him responded, bending to his will. Aquamancy, the ancient art of water manipulation, flowed through him like a long-forgotten melody. He felt the currents of Eldermere dancing at his fingertips.

In this moment of revelation, Kaelin's inner thoughts echoed the waves of emotion crashing within him. He embraced the Lumarian legacy with a newfound understanding, recognizing that each trial brought him closer to mastering the elements and unraveling the secrets of Eldermere.

## Lirael's Trial:

In a chamber adjacent to Kaelin's, Lirael faced a trial tailored to her unique connection with the elements. Lumarian symbols adorned her surroundings as she entered a state of Aetheric reverie.

## Triple Affinity Unleashed:

Lirael extended her arms, attuning herself to the ambient Aether. The triple affinity within her—air, fire, and earth—began to resonate in unison. The Lumarian Guardian's voice urged her to focus, guiding her to unlock the true potential of her elemental gifts.

As she extended her arms, attuning herself to the ambient Aether, the Lumarian Guardian's voice guided her. "Lirael, your triple affinity with air, fire, and earth is a unique convergence of elemental forces. Within this nexus, unlock the true potential of your elemental gifts."

The Aether responded to Lirael's connection with the elements. The air around her stirred, flames flickered into existence, and the earth beneath her seemed to resonate with a silent harmony. The Lumarian Guardian's whispers urged her to focus, guiding her through the Luminal secret art of Aether Magic.

## Triumph of Elemental Affinity:

As Lirael delved deeper into the Aether, a symphony of elemental forces unfolded. Cyclones of air danced around her, controlled flames swirled with grace, and the earth responded to her every step. The triple affinity, once a mysterious combination, now harmonized in a breathtaking display of elemental mastery.

## Witnessing Lumarian Legacies:

Visions manifested before Lirael, revealing her ancestors' exploits in elemental magic. The Lumarian Consortium, depicted in the statues, seemed to guide her through the ebb and flow of Aetheric currents. The Aether unveiled stories of resilience, innovation, and a shared commitment to Eldermere's magical heritage.

Yet, amid the wonder, Lirael grappled with the immense power at her fingertips. The weight of her legacy pressed upon her, creating a tension that mirrored the trials she faced. The Lumarian runes on her skin pulsed with both potential and challenge.

## Discovery of Chronicle Weaving:

As Lirael delved deeper into the Aether, her perception expanded beyond the present. With a touch, Lirael discovered a latent ability within her—Chronicle Weaving. The room flickered with echoes of forgotten tales as she wove illusions of the past and present. The Lumarian Guardian nodded in approval, recognizing the emergence of this unique skill, a tapestry that brought history to life.

The revelations unfolded like a tapestry, and Lirael realized that her triple affinity wasn't just a combination of elements—it was a conduit to the past, a connection to Eldermere's history.

## Master Elowen's Guidance:

Master Elowen, observing Lirael's trial from the ethereal realm, nodded with satisfaction. The Lumarian legacy was alive within her, and the nexus had become a canvas for the elemental symphony and the weaving of chronicles that echoed through Eldermere.

As the Lumarian Guardian's whispers faded, Lirael stood at the nexus, the elemental forces and Chronicle Weaving at her command. The trials, she realized, were not just tests of power but revelations of Lumarian legacies waiting to be unveiled.

Master Elowen, observing their trials from the nexus, nodded in approval. The Lumarian legacies were awakening within Kaelin and Lirael, and the trials were far from over. The resonance of Aetheric magic lingered in the air as the young mages continued to unravel the mysteries concealed within Eldermere's embrace.

Yet, amid the wonder, Kaelin and Lirael grappled with the immense power at their fingertips. The weight of their legacies pressed upon them, creating a tension that mirrored the trials they faced. The Lumarian runes on their skin pulsed with both potential and challenge.

# CHAPTER 8

# COALESCENCE OF CORES

After the revelations in the Lumarian Nexus, Kaelin and Lirael emerged from their respective chambers, their beings charged with newfound Aetheric prowess. Master Elowen awaited them at the nexus, a silent guide ready to reveal the next phase of their journey.

"Kaelin, Lirael," Master Elowen spoke, his voice a harmonic resonance, "the time has come to seek the magical cores that will anchor your Aetheric awakening. Within Eldermere's heart, these cores await, each attuned to the essence of Lumarian magic."

## Embarking on the Quest:

Guided by the Lumarian Guardian's whispers, the trio ventured deeper into Eldermere, where the enchanted forest whispered tales of magical cores hidden within its depths. Lumarian runes on the trees responded to their presence, forming a luminous trail that led them to a sacred glade.

## Lirael's POV:

In the glade, a mesmerizing pool of liquid Aether glistened. Around it, vibrant flora exuded Aetheric energies, creating an otherworldly aura. Lirael's triple affinity sensed the resonance, and she understood that this magical core held the essence of elemental harmony.

## Awakening the Elemental Core:

With a gesture, Lirael connected with the core. Elemental energies responded, intertwining with her triple affinity. The air, fire, and earth harmonized in a dance of luminescence, infusing the core with a unique vibrancy.

Further into the forest, Kaelin discovered a hidden cavern where the gentle murmur of running water echoed. Lumarian runes adorned the cavern walls, leading him to a radiant pool imbued with the essence of Aquamancy.

## Harmony with Aquamancy:

Kaelin approached the water, feeling a resonance with his Aquamancy. As he extended his hands, the pool responded, forming intricate patterns reminiscent of the Lumarian aquatic magic. The water became a liquid mirror, reflecting the Lumarian runes with a radiant glow.

## Master Elowen's Approval:

Master Elowen observed with a knowing smile as Kaelin and Lirael harmonized with their respective cores. "These magical cores are attuned to your unique affinities, strengthening your connection to Eldermere's magic. The time has come to weave these energies into the Lumarian Aegis."

## Weaving the Lumarian Aegis:

Guided by Master Elowen, Kaelin and Lirael channelled their Aetheric powers into the Lumarian Aegis—a manifestation of their journey, trials, and the magical cores. The Aegis shimmered with elemental brilliance, an embodiment of their Lumarian legacies.

As Kaelin and Lirael stood together, the Lumarian Aegis enveloped them in a protective aura. The forest responded to their unified power, a testament to the harmony forged through trials and the awakening of Lumarian magic.

## Master Elowen's Parting Words:

Master Elowen spoke, his voice carrying the wisdom of ages. "Kaelin, Lirael, you have harnessed the essence of Eldermere's magic. The Lumarian Aegis shall be your guide as you face the challenges that lie ahead. Your journey has only just begun."

As the Lumarian Aegis pulsed with radiant energy, Kaelin and Lirael gazed into the enchanted forest, ready to embrace the destiny woven into the fabric of Lumarian magic.

In the wake of their newfound unity with the Lumarian Aegis, Kaelin and Lirael felt a surge of determination coursing through their veins. The enchanted forest around them seemed to stir, and the whispers of Eldermere carried a cryptic message—a prelude to the challenges awaiting them.

As they delved deeper into the forest, the Lumarian Aegis guiding their way, the air became laden with mystical whispers. Shadows flitted in the corners of their vision, hinting at a hidden presence that watched their every move. Luminescent flora illuminated their path, revealing a mysterious dance of light and shadow. Strange creatures, ethereal beings that seemed to materialize from the Veil of Shadows, observed the pair with curious, otherworldly eyes.

The Lumarian Guardian's voice echoed through the forest, a cautionary melody. "Kaelin, Lirael, the Veil of Shadows conceals ancient mysteries and unforeseen dangers. Trust in the Lumarian Aegis, for it shall be your shield against the encroaching darkness." The guardian's words resonated in the air, shimmering like ripples in a pond, adding an extra layer of ethereal ambiance to the atmosphere.

## Lirael's POV:

In a clearing bathed in the soft glow of luminescent flora, Lirael noticed an ancient altar adorned with Lumarian symbols. The altar resonated with Aetheric energies, its purpose obscured by the Veil of Shadows.

## Unlocking Lumarian Secrets:

As Lirael touched the altar, visions surged forth. She glimpsed scenes of Lumarian mages unraveling secrets, performing rituals to safeguard Eldermere. The altar whispered of forgotten incantations and the need to transcend the Veil of Shadows to unveil Lumaria's hidden truths. Shimmers of translucent butterflies, creatures born of Lumarian magic, fluttered around the altar, adding a surreal quality to the mystical revelation.

## Kaelin; s POV:

In another part of the forest, Kaelin encountered a series of ancient stones inscribed with intricate runes. The stones seemed to react to the Lumarian Aegis, revealing glimpses of an impending challenge—an adversary that thrived in the Veil of Shadows.

As Kaelin focused on the stones, he entered a brief communion with the Shadow Realm. Shadows coalesced, forming vague shapes and echoes of a malevolent force. The Lumarian Guardian's warning resonated in his mind, emphasizing the importance of discerning friend from foe. Ephemeral wisps, born from the Veil of Shadows, twirled around him, creating an otherworldly dance that mirrored the intricate nature of the challenge ahead.

## Unified Vision:

Kaelin and Lirael, their visions converging, realized that the Veil of Shadows was both a gateway and a barrier. To progress in their journey, they needed to navigate the intricate threads of darkness woven into Eldermere's tapestry. The luminescent flora pulsated in unison with their realization, casting a surreal glow over the scene.

Guided by their Lumarian Aegis, Kaelin and Lirael stood at the edge of the Veil of Shadows, ready to unravel its mysteries and confront the challenges that lay beyond. The forest hushed, as if holding its breath, anticipating the outcome of their encounter with the ancient enigma. Strange creatures, shadows given form, circled around them, observing the duo with a mix of curiosity and a hint of foreboding.

# CHAPTER 9

# ECHOES OF LUMARIAN WHISPERS

## Unified Resolve:

Kaelin and Lirael, their gaze fixed on the Veil of Shadows, sensed a unity that surpassed the physical realm. The Lumarian Aegis bound them together, a luminous thread weaving through the fabric of their shared destiny. As they stepped forward, the Veil yielded, granting passage into an otherworldly expanse.

The moment their feet crossed the threshold, the forest transformed. Luminescent orbs hovered in the air, casting a gentle glow that dispersed the shadows. The Veil of Shadows, once an impediment, now revealed itself as a conduit to a realm steeped in ancient magic.

A chorus of whispers surrounded them, the voices of Lumarian mages resonating through the Veil. Each step carried echoes of forgotten incantations and tales of trials faced in the pursuit of Lumaria's arcane knowledge. The Veil itself seemed alive, responding to their presence with subtle shifts of ethereal energy.

Kaelin felt a profound connection to the element around him. It was as if the Veil acknowledged his Lumarian heritage, allowing him to discern the nuances of the Shadow Realm. Lumarian runes on his skin pulsed with newfound vigour, attuning him to the ebb and flow of the Veil's magic.

Whispers guided Kaelin through the shadowy expanse, revealing glimpses of the Lumarian Guardian's ancient trials. The path ahead intertwined with the essence of shadow magic, beckoning him to embrace its subtleties.

Lirael's perception extended beyond the present. She saw ripples in the Veil, each representing a moment in Eldermere's history. The Veil of

Shadows, she realized, was a repository of Lumarian chronicles, waiting to be unveiled through her unique ability of Chronicle Weaving.

With a touch, Lirael brought forth illusions of Lumarian mages navigating the Veil, facing trials that blurred the boundaries between reality and shadow. The Lumarian Guardian's whispers guided her, affirming the significance of her role as a chronicler of Lumarian legacies.

Kaelin and Lirael, their abilities synergizing, found themselves at a convergence point within the Veil. Lumarian symbols adorned the path ahead, shimmering with the promise of revelations. The echoes of Lumarian whispers resonated, guiding them toward an ancient chamber concealed within the Veil of Shadows.

As they entered the chamber, the Veil of Shadows retreated, revealing an enclave bathed in Aetheric luminescence. Lumarian symbols adorned the walls, and at the centre stood a pedestal with a radiant magical core—an artifact that pulsed with the essence of Lumarian magic.

The Lumarian Guardian's voice echoed within the chamber, affirming their progress. "Kaelin, Lirael, you have transcended the Veil of Shadows and stand at the heart of Lumarian knowledge. The magical core before you embodies the unity of Aether and Elemental prowess—a testament to your journey and the Lumarian legacy you carry."

Kaelin and Lirael, unified in purpose, extended their hands toward the magical core. A surge of energy enveloped them, intertwining their Aetheric and elemental affinities. The chamber resonated with harmonious luminescence as the magical core responded to the Lumarian Aegis within them.

As the magical core attuned itself to Kaelin and Lirael's combined energies, a newfound potential surged within them. The Lumarian Guardian's whispers faded, leaving them standing in the Chamber of Lumarian Echoes, ready to continue their journey with enhanced magical prowess.

As they stepped into the central plaza of Eldermere, echoes of the Lumarian Council reverberated within their consciousness. The statues that adorned the plaza seemed to come to life, each figure representing a

Lumarian mage of unparalleled expertise. The ethereal echoes carried the weight of centuries, weaving together the collective wisdom of the Lumarian Council.

## Kaelin's POV:

Kaelin, his senses heightened by the unified essence, felt a profound connection with the Lumarian Council. Their whispers guided him, revealing insights into advanced magical arts and the collective wisdom that had shaped Eldermere. Lumarian masters of different affinities—water, air, fire, earth—shared their knowledge within the ethereal council, their presence merging seamlessly with the ambient magic that permeated the air.

## Mastery Unveiled:

The Lumarian Council acknowledged Kaelin's mastery of Aquamancy and the Luminal secret art of Aether Magic. Each step he took resonated with the echoes of water and Aether, and he felt an intuitive understanding of the Lumarian techniques that went beyond what he had learned. Luminescent patterns etched into the plaza's stones glowed brighter with each mastery, illuminating the path ahead.

## Lirael's POV:

Lirael, attuned to the Veil of Shadows, perceived the Lumarian Council in a different light. Shadows enshrouded the figures, concealing and revealing ancient secrets. The Council acknowledged her compatibility of Chronicle Weaving and the intricate dance of Aether and tri element within the Veil, she glimpsed potential futures shaped by Lumarian decisions, the shifting shadows foretelling the ebb and flow of destiny.

The Lumarian Council spoke in unison, their voices a harmonious blend of elements. They revealed a *prophecy* woven into the fabric of Eldermere— the emergence of a new era guided by those who held the Lumarian Aegis. Kaelin and Lirael, as stewards of the unified essence, were destined to navigate the intricate threads of destiny. Lumarian symbols, suspended in the air, danced with ethereal energy as the *prophecy* unfolded.

United by purpose and Lumarian legacy, Kaelin and Lirael stood together in the plaza. Lumarian runes on the ground responded to their presence, glowing with the Lumarian Council's acknowledgment. The Veil of Shadows whispered of challenges and triumphs, hinting at a journey that would shape not only their destinies but the destiny of Eldermere itself. The unity of Aether and shadow radiated from them, a testament to their intertwined fates.

As they prepared to leave the central plaza, the Lumarian Council's echoes lingered. Lumarian runes etched into the statues pulsed with energy, and the air seemed charged with the Lumarian legacy. The journey ahead held the promise of unlocking further mysteries, and Kaelin and Lirael embraced the responsibility bestowed upon them by the Lumarian Council. The Lumarian echoes continued to resonate within the chamber, a reminder of the intertwined destinies that awaited them and the challenges that would shape the future of Eldermere.

# CHAPTER 10

# HARMONY OF AETHER: LUMARIAN BONDS AND THE FORGE OF DESTINY

Kaelin and Lirael stepped forth into the luminescent glow of the Lumarian Council's echoes, their skin adorned with the shimmering Lumarian runes that testified to their newfound mastery. As they embarked on the next phase of their journey, guided by the ethereal whispers resonating within them, their beings pulsated with the unified essence of Aether.

Traversing the heart of Eldermere, Lumarian bonds deepened between Kaelin and Lirael. The unified essence of Aether and elemental magic wove an unspoken language between them, each step echoing the Lumarian Aegis that bound their destinies. A seamless connection resonated through shared experiences, threading their souls in a dance of magical unity.

On the outskirts of Eldermere, where the mystical boundaries melded with untamed wilderness, Kaelin and Lirael heard ancient whispers beckoning them to the Luminal's Forge. This secluded chamber, concealed within Eldermere's heart, promised Luminal secrets of forgery that held the key to unlocking the mysteries yet undiscovered.

Lirael, attuned to the Veil of Shadows, perceived subtle energies guiding them. Shadows pirouetted along the path, revealing the way to the Luminal's Forge. Simultaneously, Kaelin felt the pull of water currents aligning with the Lumarian runes marking their route—a synchronicity of elements.

The entrance to the Luminal's Forge unveiled a mesmerizing chamber bathed in ambient light. Luminal symbols adorned the walls, and at its centre stood a Luminal—an ancient guardian of Luminal arts. The Luminal's mastery emanated, and their eyes sparkled with the depth of magical knowledge.

Welcoming Kaelin and Lirael with a nod, the Luminal acknowledged the resonance of the Lumarian Aegis. Luminal forging unfolded before their eyes—an ethereal dance of enchantment and Aetheric manipulation. Luminal symbols floated, shaping and reshaping like ethereal quills.

Kaelin, drawn to the Luminal's craft, felt the water within him respond. Aquamancy intertwined with Luminal forging, creating intricate patterns mirroring the dance of water. Meanwhile, Lirael, attuned to the Veil of Shadows, observed with keen insight as shadows melded seamlessly with Luminal symbols—a convergence of Aetheric elements.

The Luminal's voice echoed, unveiling the purpose of their encounter. Kaelin and Lirael were tasked with forging a Lumarian relic—a key unlocking Eldermere's deepest mysteries. The Luminal's ageless wisdom spoke of challenges and adversaries awaiting them in the shadows.

United by the Lumarian Aegis, Kaelin and Lirael extended their hands toward the Luminal's Forge. Aquamancy and Chronicle Weaving converged with Luminal forging, creating a Lumarian relic pulsating with the essence of their journey. The Veil of Shadows acknowledged the relic, granting it the ability to unveil hidden truths and manipulate the fabric of perception.

Empowered by the Luminal's Forge, Kaelin and Lirael emerged with newfound artifacts infused with Lumarian magic. Their Lumarian bonds resonated with the Luminal relic, a key that held the potential to unlock Eldermere's deepest mysteries.

Gathered materials, symbols, and artifacts from their journey were carefully arranged in the Luminal's Forge. The blacksmith, a skilled artisan in Lumarian crafting, awaited them. Kaelin and Lirael placed the essence-infused relics on the anvil, symbolizing the unity of their elemental affinities and magical prowess.


## Forging Process:

The blacksmith, versed in the ancient arts, channelled Aetheric currents into the materials. Lumarian symbols intertwined with the essence of water, air, fire, and earth, create a harmonious fusion. The Luminal relic took shape—a tangible representation of their journey and the Lumarian Aegis that bound them.

Kaelin, his Aquamancy attuned to the forging process, contributed the essence of water to the relic. The Aether blade, a crystalline weapon imbued with aquatic magic, materialized. His armor, woven with Luminal symbols, resonated with the ebb and flow of Eldermere's currents.

## Aetheric Enchantment:

With the Luminal relic complete, Kaelin turned to the blacksmith for Aetheric enchantment. The blacksmith, with skilled hands, channelled Aetheric energy into Kaelin's weapon and armor. Lumarian runes glowed with an intensified brilliance as the Aetheric enchantment forged a bond between Kaelin and his equipment.

## Name of the Relic: Aquaflare Tideblade Set:

Lirael, her triple affinity in full display, contributed symbols of air, fire, and earth to the Luminal relic. The Chronicle Weaving within her resonated with the crafting process, infusing the relic with the power to unveil hidden truths and manipulate illusions.

## Luminal Guidance:

The Luminal, overseeing the enchantment, guided Lirael in enhancing her equipment. Symbols representing her elemental affinities adorned a new staff, allowing her to weave illusions with unparalleled mastery. The blacksmith's Aetheric enchantment solidified the connection between Lirael and her enchanted gear.

## Name of the Relic: Elemental Weaver's Chronicle Attire:

## Unified Mastery:

Kaelin and Lirael, unified by the Lumarian relic and their individually crafted equipment, stood as embodiments of Eldermere's magic. The Aquaflare Tideblade Set and Elemental Weaver's Chronicle Attire pulsated with the Lumarian Aegis, a radiant force ready to face the challenges ahead.

The Lumarian relic, named the Aquaflare Tideblade Set and Elemental Weaver's Chronicle Attire, symbolized not only their mastery over the elements but also the unfolding chapters of Eldermere's magical tapestry

## Kaelin Wayfin:

*Class*: Aquamancer

*Kaelin specializes in water-based magic, known as Aquamancy, and has mastered the manipulation of water in various forms.*

*Weapon of Choice*: Aquaflare Tideblade

*A finely crafted blade infused with Aether and attuned to aquatic energies.*

*Armor Set*: Aquaflare Tideblade Set

*Hydrodynamic armor enhances Kaelin's agility and provides resistance against elemental attacks.*

*Passive Skill- Aquatic Harmony: Enhances Kaelin's Aquamancy by allowing him to effortlessly manipulate water in various forms. Grants increased fluidity and precision in controlling aquatic magic.*

*Unique Ability - Tide's Embrace: Upon activation, the Aquaflare Tideblade releases a surge of Aether-infused water, amplifying the power of Kaelin's strikes. It also grants temporary water-based barriers for added defense.*

*Armor Enhancement - Hydrodynamic Resonance: The armor, enchanted with Lumarian symbols, creates a protective field that attunes to Kaelin's movements. It enhances agility and provides resistance against elemental attacks.*

*Enhances Aquamancy, allowing Kaelin to effortlessly control water with increased fluidity and precision.*

## Lirael:

*Class*: Elemental Weaver

*Lirael has a triple affinity with air, fire, and earth, allowing her to weave and manipulate elemental forces with exceptional skill.*

**Weapon of Choice**: *Elemental Weaver's Chronicle Attire*

*A versatile attire attuned to Lirael's triple affinity, enhancing her control over air, fire, and earth.*

**Armor Set**: *Elemental Weaver's Chronicle Attire*

*Elemental symbols adorn the armor, providing heightened sensory perception and advanced awareness of surrounding elements.*

**Passive Ability** - *Elemental Synergy: Unlocks the full potential of Lirael's triple affinity (air, fire, earth). Enhances her ability to seamlessly weave and manipulate elemental forces.*

**Unique Ability** - *Chrono-Illusion Mastery: Activating this ability allows Lirael to weave intricate illusions of the past and present. It can disorient enemies, reveal hidden truths, and create strategic diversions on the battlefield.*

**Armor Enhancement** - *Elemental Insight: The armor, adorned with elemental symbols, heightens Lirael's sensory perception. It provides advanced awareness of the surrounding elements, enhancing her strategic acumen in battle.*

# CHAPTER 11

# THE ENIGMATIC FORGE

## Kaelin's POV:

In the heart of the Lumarian Forge, Kaelin and Lirael marvelled at the array of magical materials that surrounded them. Luminal crystals, enchanted metals, and rare gemstones sparkled in the ambient glow of Aether. The Enigmatic Smith, a master blacksmith with an air of ancient wisdom, welcomed them with a knowing smile.

"As you embark on this final phase of your journey," the Enigmatic Smith spoke, "choose wisely, for these materials will shape the essence of your relics."

## Choosing Accessories:

Before them lay an assortment of magical accessories, each radiating with unique properties. The Enigmatic Smith explained that they could only choose one each, and the accessories would enhance their innate abilities.

Kaelin, after thoughtful consideration, chose the "Tidecaller's Embrace," a magical amulet that resonated with his Aquamancy. It granted him enhanced control over water-based spells and bestowed a passive ability to harness the tides in times of need.

Lirael, with a keen understanding of her elemental affinities, chose the "Elemental Harmonium," a bracelet that harmonized her triple affinity. It allowed her to seamlessly switch between air, fire, and earth spells, amplifying the fluidity of her elemental mastery.

## Unlocking Ultimate Skills:

The Enigmatic Smith then guided them to a chamber where ancient inscriptions illuminated the walls. Here, the secrets of their ultimate skills were inscribed, waiting to be unlocked. The Enigmatic Smith explained that understanding their own power was crucial for harnessing these abilities.

Kaelin, with his newfound amulet, delved into the essence of Aquamancy. The whispers of the sea guided him as he connected with the ebb and flow of water magic. His ultimate skill, "Tidal Mastery," was a culmination of this understanding—a devastating surge of water magic that could be summoned in the most dire situations.

Lirael, attuned to the Elemental Harmonium, immersed herself in the dance of air, fire, and earth. As she comprehended the harmonious blend of her triple affinity, her ultimate skill, "Elemental Crescendo," took shape. It allowed her to unleash a symphony of elemental forces, overwhelming foes with a coordinated onslaught.

## Enchanting and Fortifying:

With their chosen accessories and unlocked ultimate skills, Kaelin and Lirael presented their relic weapons and armor to the Enigmatic Smith for enchantment and fortification.

Kaelin's Aether Blade, now named "***Aquaforged Edge***," resonated with the power of tides. The Enigmatic Smith enchanted it with Aquamancy, allowing Kaelin to summon water blades and infuse them with Aether for enhanced cutting power.

Lirael's elemental-infused armor, named "Harmony's Embrace," was fortified with Luminal crystals. The crystals enhanced her elemental control and provided added protection against magical attacks.

Kaelin, seizing the opportunity, extended his help to Lirael. With a touch of Aquamancy, he contributed to the enchantment of her armor, forging a bond between their magical affinities.

As the Enigmatic Smith completed the enchantments, Kaelin and Lirael felt the surge of power within their relics. The culmination of their journey was at hand, and the Enigmatic Smith nodded in approval as the young mages stood adorned with their enhanced relics.

## Arcane Bonds:

Kaelin's POV

Energized by the enchantments bestowed upon his Aquaforged Edge, Kaelin felt a newfound connection to the magical currents around him. As they prepared to summon their familiars, an idea sparked in his mind—an amalgamation of enchantment and conjuring magic to forge a unique entity.

Approaching an open area within the Lumarian Forge, Kaelin closed his eyes and extended his hands. Drawing upon the Aetheric energies, he envisioned a creature forged from the elements, a guardian bound to him through the intricate dance of enchantment.

## Conjuring the Elemental Guardian:

The air shimmered as Kaelin's enchantment magic intertwined with conjuring, giving rise to a magnificent Elemental Guardian. It materialized gradually, taking on ethereal forms of water, air, and luminescent energy. The Lumarian Forge resonated with the birth of this enchanted being.

As the Elemental Guardian took shape, Kaelin marvelled at the fusion of elements. Its form flowed like liquid, and within its core, a radiant luminal energy pulsed. The Lumarian Guardian's whispers echoed, acknowledging the unique bond forged through Kaelin's mastery of both enchantment and conjuring.

## Enhancing the Guardian with Aether:

With Aquaforged Edge in hand, Kaelin extended the blade toward the Elemental Guardian. The Aetheric currents from his enchanted weapon infused the guardian, amplifying its strength and imbuing it with Aquamancy. The Elemental Guardian now stood as a testament to Kaelin's dual mastery.

"I name you Aqueon, the Aetherborne Guardian," Kaelin declared, feeling the resonance of their connection. Aqueon acknowledged its name with a shimmer of approval, and together, they tested the symbiotic bond forged through enchantment, conjuring, and Aetheric enhancement.

As the Lumarian Guardian observed, a nod of acknowledgment hinted at the rarity of such a feat. Kaelin, now accompanied by Aqueon, felt a surge of confidence in the uncharted territories that awaited them.

After Kaelin's successful attempt of conjuring Aqueon, the young mage continue their never ending trial. They enter the next chamber ----------- Luminos Chamber

# CHAPTER 12

# ARCANE BONDS

**Kaelin's POV:**

In the luminous chamber, resonating with the echoes of Lumarian legacies, Kaelin and Lirael faced the task of summoning their familiars. The air crackled with magical energy as they prepared to embark on this crucial step in their journey.

Kaelin, with his proficiency in enchantment and conjuring magic, couldn't resist the idea of collaborating with Lirael. He sensed an opportunity to merge their magical prowess, creating a familiar that not only bore Lirael's essence but also resonated with the enchanting touch only he could provide.

**Offering Assistance:**

"Lirael," Kaelin said, a spark of excitement in his eyes, "what if we combine our strengths for this summoning? My enchantment magic could enhance the connection between you and your familiar, making it a unique manifestation of your magical affinity."

**Lirael's Hesitation:**

Lirael, although grateful for Kaelin's offer, hesitated. Her connection with the elements was deeply personal, and the idea of someone else influencing her summoning gave her pause. However, seeing Kaelin's genuine desire to assist, she nodded thoughtfully.

"If it means enhancing the bond with my familiar, I'm willing to try," Lirael conceded, a small smile playing on her lips.

## Enchanting the Summoning Circle:

Kaelin, with focused determination, began to weave enchantments around the summoning circle. Lumarian runes intertwined with his conjuring magic, creating an intricate web that pulsed with a dual essence—Lirael's elemental affinity and Kaelin's enchanting touch.

## Lirael's POV:

As Kaelin worked his magic, Lirael sensed the harmonious blend of their abilities. The air shimmered with anticipation, and she could feel the enchantment weaving around the magical circle, resonating with the elemental forces she sought to summon.

## Collaborative Manifestation:

The summoning reached its climax as Lirael channelled her elemental magic into the circle. The fusion of her affinity and Kaelin's enchantment created a dazzling display of magic. The familiar emerged—an ethereal creature that bore the essence of both mages, its form a testament to their collaborative effort.

## Kaelin's Enchanted Touch:

Kaelin, with a satisfied smile, extended his hand toward the familiar. His enchantment magic, now interwoven with the creature's essence, formed a subtle bond. The familiar acknowledged Kaelin's touch, its eyes glowing with a magical luminescence.

Lirael, looking at the familiar with a mix of wonder and gratitude, realized that the collaboration had resulted in something truly extraordinary. The creature radiated both elemental energy and enchanting charm, a testament to the synergy between their magical abilities.

## Kaelin's Reflection:

Kaelin, observing the familiar with a sense of accomplishment, marvelled at the successful collaboration. The enchantment added a layer of arcane intricacy to the elemental manifestation, creating a magical companion that was more than the sum of its parts.

As the magical glow subsided, Kaelin and Lirael stood together, united not only by friendship but also by the magical creation that fluttered beside them—an embodiment of their combined strengths.

In a quiet moment following the collaborative summoning, Kaelin, inspired by the bond they had forged, decided to manifest his own familiar. With a graceful gesture, he summoned forth a magnificent creature—a phoenix adorned in watery hues, dancing with ethereal flames.

Kaelin, captivated by the majestic sight, felt a connection with the creature's elemental grace. "Ignix," he whispered, naming the Aquanix Phoenix that now circled him with a regal presence. The Lumarian Guardian, observing this manifestation, nodded in silent approval as the chamber echoed with the harmonious energies of their familiars.

### Update!

*Kaelin Wayfin,*

**Class:** *Aquamancer*

**Elemental Affinity:** *Water*

**Primary Magic:** *Aether (Water and Pure Aether)*

**Unique Magic:** *Enchantment, Conjuring*

**Weapon of Choice:** *"Aquaforged Edge" previously known Aquaflare Tideblade*

*Armor Set: Aquaflare Set*

**Familiar:** *Ignix-Aquanix Phoenix*

*Skills:*

**Passive Skill:** *Aquatic Harmony*

*Enhances Aquamancy, allowing Kaelin to effortlessly control water with increased fluidity and precision.*

**Conjured Entity:** *Aqueon the Aetherborne Guardian*

*Aqueon is a sentient entity forged through the amalgamation of enchantment and conjuring magic. It serves as Kaelin's loyal companion, possessing the ability to enhance enchantments and assist in conjuring magical entities. Aqueon's presence amplifies Kaelin's proficiency in both disciplines.*

### Ultimate Skill:

### Tidal Mastery:

*A devastating surge of water magic that can be summoned in the direst situations. Tidal Mastery unleashes the full potential of Aquamancy, creating powerful tidal waves and manipulating water with unparalleled precision.*

### Equipment: Aquaflare set

### Full Set of Equipment:

### Aquaflare Helm:

*Crafted with hydrodynamic precision, enhancing aquatic affinity and providing increased visibility underwater.*

### Aquaflare Chestplate:

*Provides comprehensive protection with a hydrodynamic design that ensures flexibility and ease of movement in aquatic environments.*

### Aquaflare Gauntlets:

*Specifically designed to enhance hand movements, allowing for precise control of Aquamancy during intricate water manipulations.*

### Aquaflare Leggings:

*Offers a perfect balance of agility and protection for lower body maneuvers, facilitating swift and dynamic aquatic actions.*

### Aquaflare Boots:

*Designed to provide resilience and traction on various terrains, both underwater and on land, ensuring stability during Aquamancy rituals.*

### Tidecaller's Embrace (Accessory):

*An amulet amplifying Aquamancy, serving as a conduit to harness the tides for enhanced magical attunement. This accessory perfectly complements the Aquaflare Set, synergizing with the wearer's aquatic abilities.*

**Accessory: Tidecaller's Embrace** - *An amulet amplifying Aquamancy, serving as a conduit to harness the tides for enhanced magical attunement.*

*Lirael*

**Class:** *Elemental Weaver*

**Elemental Affinity:** *Tri Element (Air, Fire, Earth)*

**Primary Magic:** *Air, Fire, Earth*

**Unique Magic:** *Chronicle Weaving, Illusion*

**Weapon of Choice:** *Harmonyweave Scepter*

**Armor Set:** *Elemental Weaver's Chronicle Attire*

**Familiar:** *Aero - Zephyr Sentinel*

**Skills:**

**Passive Skill:** *Elemental Synergy - Unlocks Lirael's triple affinity, allowing seamless manipulation of elemental forces.*

**Equipment:** *Elemental Weaver's Chronicle Attire*

**Elemental Weaver's Garb:** *Symbols-adorned garments enhancing sensory perception and awareness.*

**Aetherfire Infused Threads:** *Enchanted threads resonating with newfound Aetheric fire, empowering Aero and providing enhanced magical protection.*

*Sensory Enigma Hood: A hood that intensifies Lirael's perception, allowing her to weave illusions with heightened clarity.*

**Harmonyweave Sleeves:** *Sleeves woven with harmonious threads, amplifying the precision of elemental control.*

**Aegisweave Shroud:** *A shimmering shroud that grants additional protection and agility in the heat of battle.*

**Chroniclestep Boots:** *Boots crafted with Lumarian symbols, enabling swift and silent movement for precise positioning during illusion weaving.*

**Accessory: Elemental Harmonium:**

*A bracelet harmonizing Lirael's triple affinity.*

*Enables seamless switching between air, fire, and earth spells.*

*Amplifies elemental mastery.*

# CHAPTER 13

# GOLEM'S LAST STAND

Enveloped within the protective embrace of the Lumarian Aegis, Kaelin and Lirael felt an electrifying surge coursing through their veins. The magical field heightened their senses, and the ambient Aether seemed to respond to their presence more readily. The Luminal runes on their skin shimmered with an intensified luminosity, a visible manifestation of the boosted connection with Aether.

Choosing Accessories: In the midst of this heightened state, the selection of magical accessories took on a profound resonance. Kaelin, attuned to the amplified flow of Aether, found the decision-making process more intuitive. The "Tidecaller's Embrace" seemed to resonate with an even deeper connection, promising an enhanced mastery over Aquamancy as he envisioned the ebb and flow of tides with newfound clarity.

Lirael, with her triple elemental affinity, could sense the harmonious dance of Aether within the "Elemental Harmonium." The Lumarian Aegis allowed her to grasp the intricate balance between air, fire, and earth elements, making the choice feel like a natural extension of her heightened connection with the magical essence.

Unlocking Ultimate Skills: Guided by the Lumarian Aegis, Kaelin immersed himself in the essence of Aquamancy. The whispers of the sea became a symphony, resonating in harmony with the Aether that surrounded him. The ultimate skill, "Tidal Mastery," took on an even more potent form, the Aegis amplifying its cataclysmic potential.

Lirael, her senses heightened by the Lumarian Aegis, delved into the elemental forces with unprecedented clarity. The ultimate skill, "Elemental Crescendo," unfolded as a majestic symphony, each elemental note resonating with the intensified Aether, creating an overwhelming barrage of harmonized magic.

Enchanting and Fortifying: Within the Aetheric cocoon, Kaelin and Lirael presented their relics to the Enigmatic Smith. The magical materials responded with increased receptivity, allowing for a more profound enchanting and fortifying process.

Kaelin's "Aquaforged Edge," now synergizing seamlessly with the Lumarian Aegis, received enchantments that went beyond the ordinary. The Luminal crystals responded to the Aetheric boost, creating a blade that could not only cut through physical barriers but also disrupt magical defenses with Aetheric resonance.

Lirael's "Harmony's Embrace" absorbed Luminal energies with heightened efficiency. The Aegis enhanced the protective qualities of the armor, forming an ethereal shield that could deflect not only physical attacks but also disrupt hostile magical energies.

Aetheric Synergy: United in their Aetheric empowerment, Kaelin and Lirael marvelled at the resonance between their relics and the Lumarian Aegis. The Lumarian runes on their skin glowed with an ethereal brilliance, a visual testament to the harmonious synergy between their enhanced magical abilities and the omnipresent Aetheric energy.

As they stepped away from the Lumarian Forge, embraced by the lingering Lumarian Aegis, Kaelin and Lirael felt a profound connection not only with each other but with the very fabric of Eldermere itself. The Aetheric boost had not only elevated their magical prowess but had forged a link that transcended the physical and mystical realms, setting the stage for the challenges that awaited them in their quest.


## Kaelin'POV:

With their enhanced relics and newly summoned familiars, Kaelin and Lirael ventured deeper into the Lumarian Forge. Their journey brought them to a vast chamber where an ancient golem, powered by Aetheric energies, awaited them as the final trial.

The golem, a towering colossus of enchanted stone, emanated a formidable presence. Lumarian symbols glowed on its surface, and Aetheric currents pulsed within its core. It stood as the guardian of the forge, a testament to the challenges that awaited any mage seeking mastery.

## Facing the Golem:

Kaelin and Lirael exchanged determined glances, their newfound confidence radiating from the relics that adorned them. Aquanix Phoenix and Zephyr Sentinel, the summoned familiars, circled protectively as if sensing the impending challenge.

With a nod of silent agreement, they advanced toward the golem, its eyes glowing with an otherworldly light. The air crackled with anticipation as the golem came to life, massive limbs shifting into a combat stance.

## Lirael's POV:

Lirael felt the resonance of her Elemental Weaver's Chronicle Attire, the symbols glowing brighter in response to the approaching threat. Aero, her summoned familiar, coiled with readiness, mirroring her determination to overcome the formidable foe.

As they closed in on the golem, the air around Lirael stirred with elemental energy. She extended her arms, ready to unleash the symphony of elemental forces that now obeyed her command.

## Unified Assault:

Kaelin, with Aquaforged Edge in hand, summoned Aqueon, the Aetherborne Guardian. The elemental entity moved with aquatic grace, aligning itself with Kaelin's focused intent. The Aquaflare Tideblade set pulsed with power as Aqueon and Kaelin prepared for their assault. Thousands of water droplet emerge from his surroundings combining with the essence of aether in the air making the water droplet into a deadly projectile that fires at the golem

Lirael, with Elemental Crescendo at her disposal, unleashed a coordinated barrage of air, fire, and earth magic. Aero's movements intertwined seamlessly with Lirael's spells, creating a mesmerizing dance of elements. Her mastery over the element made the magical output more intense than usual.

The golem, formidable as it was, struggled to withstand the combined onslaught. Water blades and water projectile collided with fiery eruptions, and the very earth beneath trembled with the force of their attack.

## Kaelin's POV:

As the battle unfolded, Kaelin marvelled at the synergy between their abilities. Aquanix Phoenix, his newly summoned familiar, soared through the elemental chaos, its watery flames complementing the vibrant display of magic. The Tidecaller's Embrace amulet responded to Kaelin's will, enhancing the aquatic aspects of their assault.

## Triumph and Unity:

With a final, coordinated strike, Kaelin and Lirael overcame the ancient golem. The enchanted stone crumbled, its Aetheric core dispersing like fading echoes. The chamber, once filled with the clash of magic and stone, fell into a profound silence.

## POV - Master Elowen:

Master Elowen, appearing before them in the aftermath of their victory, nodded with a sense of satisfaction. Lumarian symbols glowed on his robes, resonating with the relics worn by Kaelin and Lirael.

With a gesture, he beckoned both Kaelin and Lirael to approach. The pair, marked by the trials they had faced, stood before their mentor. A smile played on Master Elowen's lips as he acknowledged their shared triumph over the elemental challenges.

"Kaelin, Lirael," he spoke with a tone that echoed both approval and warmth, "your journey through Aquamancy and Elemental Weaving has proven fruitful. The waters and elements have responded to your command. Your growth is evident, and I commend you both."

"You have faced the trials of the Lumarian Forge with unity and mastery," Master Elowen praised, his voice echoing in the chamber. "Your collaboration, the forging of relics, and the summoning of familiars have proven your readiness to carry the Lumarian legacy forward."

He extended a hand, encompassing them both in his wise gaze. "Rest now, for tomorrow brings new horizons and challenges. Your unity in the trials has not gone unnoticed, and together, you shall weave a narrative of strength and harmony for Eldermere."

## Acknowledgment and Beyond:

Kaelin and Lirael, standing side by side, exchanged glances infused with mutual respect and accomplishment. The trials had tested not only their magical prowess but also their ability to collaborate and support each other.

"As you step beyond the forge, remember that your journey has just begun," Master Elowen continued. "The Lumarian legacy is not just a path of power but one of understanding, unity, and the continual pursuit of magical excellence."

With those words, the Lumarian Forge's ancient symbols glowed one last time, and the chamber resonated with a harmonious energy. As the glow subsided, Kaelin and Lirael found themselves at the entrance of the forge, ready to embark on the next chapter of their magical journey.

As they withdrew to embrace the well-deserved respite, Master Elowen watched, knowing that the tapestry of their magical journey had only just begun to unfold.

## Master Elowen, the Aether Conjurer:

*Title:* *The Aether Conjurer*

*Elemental Affinity:* *Aether (Connected to all basic elements)*

*Primary Magic :* *Aether-based Enchantment, Conjuring, and Aetherial Weaving*

*Unique Magic:* *Aetherial Nexus Mastery*

*Weapon:* *Aetherial Scepter*

*Familiar:* *Aetherial Phoenix*

*Conjured Entity:* *Ethereal Guardians*

## Skills:

**Aetherial Enchantment**: Mastery in infusing objects with ethereal energies, enhancing properties, or imbuing magical effects.

**Conjuration of the Aether Realm:** Ability to summon manifestations from the Aether Realm, creating illusions, shields, or ethereal allies.

## Passive Skills:

**Aetherial Attunement:** Innate understanding of Aether magic, enabling the sensing of disturbances and foreseeing potential threats.

**Ethereal Weaving:** Skill in dynamically manipulating Aetheric energies, allowing the morphing of appearance and enhancing magical resonance.

## Ultimate Magic:

**Aetherial Ascendance:** Attaining immense magical power by attuning with the converging energies of the Aether Realm during a celestial alignment, enabling brief transcendence and unprecedented Aether manipulation.

## Equipment:

**Aetherial Robes:** Enchanted robes enhancing magical focus and providing protection against Aetheric disturbances.

**Aetherborne Amulet:** An amulet infused with Aetherial essence, amplifying Aetheric attunement and providing a link to the Aether Realm.

**Ethereal Circlet:** A crystalline circlet aiding in ethereal weaving, allowing for intricate manipulation of Aetheric energies.

**Celestial Staff:** A staff adorned with Lumarian symbols, serving as a conduit for Aetherial magic and enhancing the effectiveness of enchantments.

**Aetherial Nexus Stone:** A crystalline stone acting as a focal point for Aetherial rituals, enhancing the summoning of entities from the Aether Realm and manifesting the unique magic of Aetherial Nexus Mastery.

# CHAPTER 14

# VEILED MACHINATIONS

***This event happened at the same time as Kaelin's and Lirael's trial*:**

Aric stood on the threshold of the forbidding Voidshaper Sanctum, its reputation veiled in secrecy. The atmosphere inside was dense with an otherworldly aura, and as Aric advanced, the shadows clung to him, whispering ancient incantations that resonated through the vast chamber. Illuminated symbols adorned the walls, each flicker inviting him to embrace the enigmatic teachings of the Voidshapers.

Guided deeper into the sanctum, Aric encountered Master Voss, the mysterious Voidshaper instructor draped in shadows. Voss's piercing gaze penetrated Aric's core as he acknowledged the young seeker's quest for the path of shadows. Under Voss's tutelage, Aric underwent intense training, his innate magic responding to the esoteric arts of Voidshaping.

Weeks unfolded as Aric delved into the mysteries of the void. He mastered the manipulation of shadows, learned to cloak his presence, and discovered the secrets of void portals and astral projections from ancient scrolls. In a pivotal moment during a celestial alignment, Aric harnessed the converging energies, achieving the revered Voidwalker class.

With his newfound class, Aric became a master of traversing the void, seamlessly stepping between dimensions. The shadows became his allies, responding to his every command. However, the acquisition of these powers left an indelible mark on Aric. The equilibrium between light and darkness within him became delicate, hinting at both potential and peril on the unfolding path.

Meanwhile, as Kaelin and Lirael faced their trials in Aquamancy and Elemental Weaving, Aric's journey into the shadows hinted at a destiny intertwined with the intricate dance between light and darkness—a path that held secrets yet to be unveiled.

As Aric delved deeper into the mysteries of Voidshaping under Master Voss's guidance, a clandestine plot unfolded in the shadows of the forbidding sanctum. Unbeknownst to Aric, his mentor harboured dark ambitions that transcended the mere passing of knowledge.

Master Voss, draped in shadows, observed Aric's progress with an intensity that went beyond mentorship. In the recesses of his mind, he saw not just a skilled practitioner, but a vessel—a conduit through which he could attain unprecedented power. Whispers from the void promised ascendance, and Voss couldn't resist the allure of merging with Aric to unleash chaos upon Eldermere.

In the dimly lit sanctum, the shadows seemed to dance with malevolent glee as Voss envisioned his dominion. Yet, amidst his dark contemplations, an unexpected observer lurked. Voss's own consort, a defector from the Luminary Consortium, moved silently in the shadows. Overhearing the whispers of Voss's malevolent plans, she understood the impending threat to Eldermere and swore to prevent history from repeating itself.

The consort, once part of the Consortium apprentice but now an enigmatic figure working against Voss, had her own motives. Her true allegiance lay with the former vessel of Master Voss—a puppet master orchestrating events from afar. As Voss plotted to merge with Aric, the consort vowed to thwart him, setting the stage for a clandestine battle of wills within the shadows.

In the sanctum's depths, alliances and betrayals unfolded, each step taken in the dance of fate bringing Eldermere closer to the precipice. As Aric honed his skills, unaware of the looming threat, the shadows held secrets that would shape the destiny of the realm.


### *Recap of the current story*

While Aric immersed himself in the shadows of the Voidshaper Sanctum, Kaelin and Lirael continued their arduous trials in the realms of Aquamancy and Elemental Weaving.

As Kaelin delved into the intricate control of water, each trial tested the limits of his Aquamancy. The resonance of crashing waves and the fluidity of his magic intertwined, creating a symphony of power. Meanwhile, Lirael wove elemental forces with grace, each thread of magic responding to her every command.

Unbeknownst to them, in the shadows that concealed the forbidden secrets of the Voidshapers, Aric's journey unfolded, setting the stage for a convergence of destinies yet to be revealed.

As Kaelin and Lirael navigate through their elemental trials, they discover a hidden synergy between Aquamancy and Elemental Weaving. The magical energies resonate, creating a unique confluence that draws the attention of Eldermere's mystical beings.

In their respective challenges, Kaelin finds himself immersed in a magical pool, where water responds to the ebb and flow of his Aquamancy. Lirael, on the other hand, encounters an ethereal grove where the elements dance to her command, intertwining in an intricate display of Elemental Weaving.

As the two companions progress, they begin to sense a connection beyond their individual trials. Unseen forces guide their actions, hinting at a larger design that involves the very fabric of Eldermere's elemental balance.

Simultaneously, Aric's journey within the shadows takes an unexpected turn as he stumbles upon cryptic clues that tie his fate to the confluence of Kaelin and Lirael's elemental powers.

# CHAPTER 15

# THREADS OF REFLECTION

The aftermath of the elemental trials left Kaelin and Lirael in reflective silence, each caught in the intricate dance of their thoughts as they retired to their chambers.

In his quiet quarters, Kaelin wielded his Aquaforged Edge, not just as a tool for magic but as a companion in contemplation. The resonance of his battle with the ancient golem echoed within him, interwoven with Master Elowen's advice to rest. Yet, amid the silence, another resonance lingered — the memory of their synchronized magic, a connection forged in the elemental symphony.

Across the sanctum, Lirael found solace in the gentle glow of her familiar, Aero, the Zephyr Sentinel. Its warmth provided a stark contrast to the cool calculations of her thoughts. The enhancements Kaelin had bestowed upon her equipment played like a melody in her mind. The truth asserted itself — a connection had formed, entwining their magical journeys.

Denying her feelings became an act of quelling a tempest with a whisper. With each heartbeat, the denial waned, and the truth asserted itself. She recalled Kaelin's presence during the summoning, the harmonious dance of their magic resonating in the elemental symphony.

As sleep embraced them, dreams manifested, bringing fragments of memories. In shared dreamscape fragments, Lirael saw echoes of her parents, their voices entwining with the unspoken threads of her heart. The dream hinted at acceptance — the acceptance of her feelings for Kaelin as an integral part of her magical essence.

With the dawn of a new day, a subtle shift had occurred. The elements whispered ancient secrets, and in that shared understanding, a silent vow echoed — to navigate the uncertainties together, bound by the threads of shared magic and weaving hearts. The symphony of their connection played on, weaving a tale that transcended the elemental trials.

With the first light of dawn casting a warm embrace, Master Elowen found himself lost in contemplation within the Lumarian Sanctum. The trials faced by his pupils lingered in the air like an echo of the past, awakening memories both cherished and solemn.

A gentle breeze carried with it an unexpected guest—Eldarion, an old friend and Lumarian comrade. Eldarion's mastery over formidable and unique magical abilities made him a respected figure among his peers, a Lumarian who had carved a different path in the pursuit of knowledge.

"Elowen, my old friend," Eldarion greeted warmly, the wisdom of years reflected in his smile. "Whispers reached me of the trials your pupils endured. It seems the Lumarian legacy endures within these walls."

Acknowledging the shared history, Elowen replied, "Eldarion, your timing is impeccable. The young ones have faced challenges that tested their mettle. Join me, and let us share the tales of their elemental journeys."

As they wandered through the sanctum, Elowen recounted the trials of Kaelin, Lirael, and their experiences in mastering the elements. Eldarion listened attentively, his gaze reflecting an understanding that transcended the words spoken.

Immersed in conversation, the Lumarian friends traversed the corridors of memory, where tales of the past intermingled with uncertainties of the future. Eldarion's presence hinted at the interconnected threads of magic weaving through Eldermere, transcending the boundaries of individual legacies.

As the stories unfolded, Eldarion's expression grew somber. "Elowen, I carry a regret that has weighed on my heart since that fateful day when the void threatened our realm. My pursuit of knowledge led me astray, and I was absent when you needed every Lumarian by your side."

Elowen, understanding the depth of Eldarion's remorse, nodded solemnly. "The past cannot be rewritten, my friend. We faced the void and emerged victorious. But your willingness to stand with us now speaks volumes. The trials are not over, and Eldermere may yet need the strength of Lumarians united."

Eldarion's eyes gleamed with a newfound resolve. "Elowen, grant me the chance to redeem myself in the battles to come. I stand ready to lend my magic and my strength to safeguard Eldermere from any threat that may arise."

Elowen clasped Eldarion's shoulder with gratitude. "Your loyalty and resolve have never wavered, my friend. In the battles that lie ahead, your presence will be a beacon of Lumarian unity. Together, we shall face whatever shadows may come."

## Later that day:

In the sacred confines of the Lumarian Sanctum, as the resonance of memories lingered, Master Elowen felt the time was ripe to call upon his ethereal allies. With a commanding presence, he invoked the ancient incantations that bound him to two remarkable entities—the Aetherial Phoenix and the Ethereal Guardians.

From the veil between realms emerged the majestic Aetherial Phoenix, its feathers aflame with ethereal hues. Simultaneously, the Ethereal Guardians materialized, their forms composed of radiant energy and Lumarian symbols.

Yet, unlike their usual solemn welcomes, a mischievous spark ignited in the eyes of the Aetherial Phoenix and the Ethereal Guardians. In a coordinated, playful dance, they attempted a light-hearted prank on their revered master, attempting to catch him off guard.

The Aetherial Phoenix, with playful flames flickering, teased, "Ah, Master Elowen, it seems an eternity since you summoned us together. Have we become mere myths in the pages of Lumarian lore?"

The Ethereal Guardians joined in, their energy shimmering with amusement. "Indeed, Master Elowen, the ethereal realms yearned for our reunion. Shall we initiate a playful welcome, a dance of jests to mark this long-overdue summoning?"

Master Elowen, ever attuned to the nuances of his ethereal allies, gracefully sidestepped their attempted pranks with a knowing smile. "My dear allies, your playful spirit warms my heart. It has been too long, and your presence is a balm to the sanctum's echoes."

With a graceful acknowledgment of their master's evasion, the Aetherial Phoenix and the Ethereal Guardians ceased their antics. A sense of camaraderie filled the sanctum, their ethereal presence blending seamlessly with the magical currents.

Regaining their composure, the Aetherial Phoenix spoke with a regal tone, "Master, we have watched over Eldermere in your absence. The threads of magic speak of void disturbances in the recent trials. The Voidshapers, ancient and elusive, have left their mark."

The Ethereal Guardians, ever vigilant, added, "Master Elowen, fear not, for we shall keep a watchful eye on your pupils. Their trials have unveiled new strengths, but the looming shadows call for strategic vigilance."

Master Elowen, appreciating their loyalty, apologized for the prolonged separation and offered their favourite ethereal treats as a token of reconciliation. As the ethereal entities partook in their favourite essence-infused delights, a council formed within the sanctum—a meeting of Lumarian and ethereal minds to strategize against the encroaching darkness. In the shared moments, the sanctuary pulsed with the unity of realms, preparing for the challenges that lay ahead.

As the Aetherial Phoenix and Ethereal Guardians basked in the familiar ambiance of the Lumarian Sanctum, a peculiar realization dawned upon them. Their ethereal senses, finely attuned to the threads of magical essence, detected an uncanny resonance with the creatures summoned and conjured by Kaelin Wayfin.

Curiosity gleamed in the eyes of the Aetherial Phoenix as it gracefully addressed Master Elowen, "Master, the beings conjured by your pupil, Kaelin Wayfin, bear a semblance to our ethereal existence. Their magical resonance echoes across the realms. Could you enlighten us about their nature?"

Master Elowen, a custodian of ancient knowledge, wore a contemplative expression. "Ah, my esteemed allies, the time for a complete introduction has not yet arrived. The threads of fate are intricately woven, and the revelation of their true nature must unfold at its destined moment. For now, let us observe and safeguard the balance."

Understanding the cryptic response, the Ethereal Guardians nodded in agreement. Their luminous forms exuded an air of patience, acknowledging the intricate dance of destiny.

However, the perceptive Aetherial Phoenix, its flames flickering with insight, directed its gaze toward Lirael's Zephyr Sentinel. "Master Elowen, I sense a unique essence within the Zephyr Sentinel, Lirael's loyal companion. There is an endangered aura, a potential to unlock an evolution that could safeguard its ethereal kin. Have you observed this, Master?"

Master Elowen, attuned to the delicate balance of magical essences, nodded in acknowledgment. "Indeed, my radiant ally. The Zephyr Sentinel bears a special trait, a key to unlocking a new evolution. In the intricate tapestry of magical species, its potential to safeguard and evolve may hold the key to the preservation of endangered ethereal beings."

With this revelation, a shared understanding permeated the sanctum—a delicate connection between Lumarian and ethereal entities, intertwined with the destinies of those who tread the mystical path. As the Aetherial Phoenix and Ethereal Guardians continued their vigilant watch, the threads of fate whispered of mysteries yet to unfold, weaving a narrative that transcended realms.

# CHAPTER 16

# AETHERIAL MASTERY UNVEILED

In the luminous expanse of the Lumarian Sanctum, the Aetherial Phoenix spread its majestic wings, its plumage shimmering with ethereal radiance. With a graceful dance in the air, the phoenix began to weave an intricate pattern of magical threads, channeling its refined skills into the creation of an extraordinary barrier.

As the ethereal barrier took shape, it manifested as a shimmering veil encircling the sanctum and extend the barrier's range throughout Eldermere. Master Elowen observed in awe as the Aetherial Phoenix, with each beat of its wings, embedded an alerting enchantment within the barrier. This magical lattice, attuned to the subtle disturbances in the air, would serve as a sentinel, instantly notifying Master Elowen of any disruptions or intrusions.

The phoenix, its eyes gleaming with ancient wisdom, turned to Master Elowen and conveyed, "Master, this barrier shall resonate with the very essence of air. It shall remain vigilant, echoing disturbances through the threads of magic. A guardian to protect the sanctum from unseen threats."

Meanwhile, the Ethereal Guardians manifested their ethereal forms amidst the elemental sanctuaries within the Lumarian city. With a harmonious blend of magical incantations, they summoned golems of every natural element — earth, water, fire, and air. These elemental sentinels, hewn from the essence of the natural world, stood as silent protectors of the city.

The earth golem, sturdy and resilient, took its place near the entrance, while the water golem, fluid and agile, patrolled the waterways surrounding the sanctuaries. The fire golem, with flames dancing in controlled fury, stood as a beacon of protection, and the air golem, ethereal and swift, soared above, vigilant in the skies.

Master Elowen, witnessing this breathtaking display of ethereal mastery, acknowledged the importance of these enchanted guardians. "Your skills, dear allies, weave a tapestry of safeguarding the sanctum and the city. The Lumarian realms are indebted to your watchful presence."

With the ethereal barrier alerting to disturbances and the elemental golems standing sentinel, the Lumarian Sanctum embraced an enhanced layer of protection, a testament to the collaborative efforts of Lumarian and ethereal entities. As the threads of magic and ethereal essence intertwined, the sanctum stood as a bastion against the unseen forces that lurked in the mystical realms.

## Conjuring Anew:

Master Elowen, The Aether Conjurer, stood at the heart of the Lumarian Sanctum, surrounded by the ethereal glow of magical incantations. His Aetherial Phoenix and Ethereal Guardians, faithful companions in the dance of magic, prepared for the creation of a new entity born of aether.

"In the symphony of our shared magic, let us weave a companion that embodies the essence of Aetherial Nexus Mastery," declared Master Elowen, the resonance of his words echoing through the sanctum.

The Aetherial Phoenix, with wings aglow, and the Ethereal Guardians, embodiments of elemental forces, joined their energies. Master Elowen, wielding his Aetherial Scepter, began the intricate dance of conjuration, each movement weaving the threads of aether into existence.

As the ritual unfolded, the Aetherial Nexus Stone at the centre of the sanctum emanated a radiant aura, acting as a focal point for the convergence of magical energies. The newly conjured entity emerged, a harmonious fusion of Lumarian and ethereal magic, bearing the unique essence of Aetherial Nexus Mastery.

This ethereal being, an embodiment of magical intricacies, stood beside the Aetherial Phoenix and Ethereal Guardians, forming a trio of enchanting protectors. Its presence resonated with the Aetherial Conjurer's gratitude, a testament to the collaborative efforts of Lumarian and ethereal entities in crafting this new companion.

With a nod of acknowledgment, Master Elowen named the conjured entity, "Aetherial Nexus Warden," signifying its role as a guardian and a nexus of aetheric energies. The Aetherial Phoenix and Ethereal Guardians, delighted with the addition to their magical family, playfully demonstrated the new entity's capabilities.

As a gesture of appreciation, Master Elowen thanked his ethereal companions, and the trio, now united in purpose, prepared to fulfill their roles as guardians of the Lumarian Sanctum. The Aetherial Nexus Warden, born of shared magic and ancient bonds, embraced its purpose, ready to embark on a journey alongside its Lumarian creators.

## Master Elowen, The Aether Conjurer:

*Title:* The Aether Conjurer

*Elemental Affinity:* Aether (Connected to all basic elements)

*Primary Magic:* Aether-based Enchantment, Conjuring, and Aetherial Weaving

*Unique Magic:* Aetherial Nexus Mastery

*Weapon:* Aetherial Scepter

*Familiar:* Aetherial Phoenix

*Conjured Entity:* Ethereal Guardians

## New Addition:

*Aetherial Nexus Warden:* Through collaborative efforts with his familiar, the Aetherial Phoenix, and the Ethereal Guardians, Master Elowen has recently conjured a new entity, the Aetherial Nexus Warden. This enchanting guardian embodies the essence of Aetherial Nexus Mastery and stands as a testament to the harmonious collaboration between Lumarian and ethereal entities.

## Skills:

*Aetherial Enchantment:* Mastery in infusing objects with ethereal energies, enhancing properties, or imbuing magical effects.

***Conjuration of the Aether Realm:*** *Ability to summon manifestations from the Aether Realm, creating illusions, shields, or ethereal allies.*

***Aetherial Nexus Mastery:*** *Channeling the converging energies of the Aether Realm, Master Elowen can create, manipulate, and control the unique magical essence known as Aetherial Nexus. This skill allows him to forge powerful connections between magical entities, facilitating the creation of the Aetherial Nexus Warden.*

## Passive Skills:

***Aetherial Attunement:*** *Innate understanding of Aether magic, enabling the sensing of disturbances and foreseeing potential threats.*

***Ethereal Weaving:*** *Skill in dynamically manipulating Aetheric energies, allowing the morphing of appearance and enhancing magical resonance.*

## Ultimate Magic:

***Aetherial Ascendance:*** *Attaining immense magical power by attuning with the converging energies of the Aether Realm during a celestial alignment, enabling brief transcendence and unprecedented Aether manipulation.*

## Equipment:

***Aetherial Robes:*** *Enchanted robes enhancing magical focus and providing protection against Aetheric disturbances.*

***Aetherborne Amulet:*** *An amulet infused with Aetherial essence, amplifying Aetheric attunement and providing a link to the Aether Realm.*

***Ethereal Circlet:*** *A crystalline circlet aiding in ethereal weaving, allowing for intricate manipulation of Aetheric energies.*

***Celestial Staff:*** *A staff adorned with Lumarian symbols, serving as a conduit for Aetherial magic and enhancing the effectiveness of enchantments.*

***Aetherial Nexus Stone:*** *A crystalline stone acting as a focal point for Aetherial rituals, enhancing the summoning of entities from the Aether Realm and manifesting the unique magic of Aetherial Nexus Mastery.*

# CHAPTER 17

# AETHERIAL REVELATIONS

As the Lumarian Sanctum basks in the enchanting aftermath of the conjuration ritual, a ripple in the magical fabric alerts Master Elowen. The Aetherial Nexus Warden, Aetherial Phoenix, and Ethereal Guardians sense a disturbance—a subtle shift in the threads of destiny.

Master Elowen, guided by his attunement to Aether, discovers an ancient *prophecy* hidden within the Lumarian archives. The *prophecy* hints at an impending convergence of elemental forces and a looming threat that could unravel the delicate balance of magic.

Intrigued and concerned, Master Elowen gathers Kaelin, Lirael, and their allies to decipher the *prophecy*. As they delve into ancient texts and arcane symbols, the threads of destiny weave tales of trials, alliances, and an ancient artifact that holds the key to averting the impending catastrophe.

Meanwhile, shadows stir in the Voidshaper Sanctum, echoing the disturbances in the magical realms. Aric, now a master of Voidwalking, senses the tremors and embarks on a quest to uncover the truth behind the ancient *prophecy*, inadvertently crossing paths with a figure from Eldermere's forgotten past.

Together, they poured over the ancient tomes, the symbols resisting easy interpretation. The threads of destiny intricately woven in the *prophecy* eluded their understanding. In a moment of realization, Master Elowen acknowledged the need for a specialist in ancient languages.

Summoning Eldarion, the Aetherial Archeologist, became the logical choice. Eldarion, with a class specifically attuned to deciphering ancient texts and a mastery over an advanced form of Chronicle Weaving, was the Lumarian's foremost expert in unraveling the secrets of the past.

As Eldarion arrived, a faint glow surrounded him, a testament to the Aetherial Nexus Mastery that infused his archaeological expertise. With precision, he examined the Lumarian script, his skill allowing him to delve into the very fabric of the past without altering the present.

The Lumarian language unfolded before Eldarion's gaze, and with each revelation, the *prophecy's* meaning began to emerge. Threads of destiny connected the past to the present, weaving a narrative of elemental convergence, ancient alliances, and a looming threat that could reshape Eldermere's magical landscape.

The deciphered *prophecy* hinted at an artifact, a relic of immense power, hidden in the heart of Eldermere. To avert the impending catastrophe, the group would need to embark on a quest that traversed the realms of magic, unlocking the true potential of their elemental affinities.

With the *prophecy* unveiled, the characters found themselves at the crossroads of destiny. The Lumarian Sanctum, resonating with the threads of ancient magic, became the starting point for a journey that would test their bonds and unveil the intricate tapestry of Eldermere's destiny.

The revelation of Eldarion's advanced skills hung in the air like a charged enchantment. Lirael, her eyes widened in awe, found herself marvelling at the intricate dance of Eldarion' s magic—a dance that resonated with her own but possessed an unparalleled depth.

Later, as the trio made their way back to their chambers, Eldarion observed Lirael closely. He noticed an inherent connection to the Aether, a dormant potential that mirrored his quad elemental affinity. Curiosity piqued, he approached Lirael, "You, too, possess a remarkable set of powers, similar to mine but with a unique touch. The Aether flows through you in ways I find intriguing."

Master Elowen, ever insightful, saw an opportunity for Lirael to delve into the depths of her magical prowess. Gathering the trio in a quiet corridor, he proposed a unique mentorship. "Lirael," he began, "your mastery over the elements is commendable, but Eldarion here possesses a unique expertise in advanced Chronicle Weaving, a skill that aligns with your own magical abilities."

Eldarion, the Aetherial Archaeologist, acknowledged Lirael's potential. "Indeed, your prowess in the tri-elements is remarkable. However, I sense a latent power within you, a potential for a greater version of Chronicle Weaving. Together, we can explore the intricacies of this ancient art."

Lirael, both humbled and intrigued, welcomed the opportunity to learn from Eldarion. Master Elowen continued, "Consider Eldarion your mentor in the art of advanced Chronicle Weaving. His mastery in deciphering ancient languages and temporal manipulation will unveil new horizons in your magical journey."

Lirael, though unsure of the extent of her abilities, welcomed the opportunity to explore the depths of her magic. Master Elowen, recognizing the potential for an extraordinary collaboration, envisioned a future where Lumarian and Aetherial magic intertwined seamlessly.

Eldarion, with a smile that mirrored his eagerness to share his knowledge, added, "We shall embark on a journey of discovery, unlocking the full extent of your magical abilities. The echoes of the past hold secrets, and with your affinity for the elements, we can weave a narrative that transcends time itself."

As the trio ventured into uncharted territories of ancient prophecies and mystical powers, a sense of anticipation lingered. The unspoken bond between Lirael and Eldarion hinted at a destiny woven with threads of shared magic—an alliance that would play a pivotal role in the unfolding tale of Eldermere. The echoes of their footsteps resonated through the sanctum, marking the beginning of a new chapter in their magical journey.

And so, a new chapter unfolded for Lirael as Eldarion took her under his wing. Together, they would explore the realms of advanced Chronicle Weaving, pushing the boundaries of magic and unraveling the ancient threads that connected their destinies.

## Eldarion, The Aetherial Archeologist:

*Title: Aetherial Archeologist*

*Elemental Affinity: Quad Element (Fire, Water, Earth, Air)*

*Primary Magic: Elemental Mastery, Summoning Magic*

*Unique Magic: Aetherial Nexus Mastery, Advanced Chronicle Weaving,*

*Class*: Aetherial Archeologist

*Familiar*: Ethereal Scholar (Quad Elemental)

## Skills:

**Advanced Chronicle Weaving:** *Eldarion can weave intricate illusions, access historical events through the Aetherial Nexus, and even glimpse into the past without altering the present.*

**Elemental Mastery:** *Proficient control over Fire, Water, Earth, and Air magic, allowing Eldarion to harness the unique properties of each element.*

**Summoning Prowess:** *Eldarion can summon ethereal entities and elemental beings from the past to aid him in deciphering ancient mysteries or confronting adversaries.*

**Linguistic Insight:** *Eldarion possesses an innate understanding of ancient languages, allowing him to decipher cryptic scripts and unravel the secrets of the past.*

**Aetherial Attunement:** *Eldarion can sense disturbances in Aether, aiding in the identification of magical anomalies or hidden artifacts.*

**Elemental Fusion:** *Eldarion can merge elemental energies to create powerful combinations, enhancing the effectiveness of his magic.*

**Aetherial Resonance:** *Eldarion can attune himself to the ambient Aether, granting heightened magical perception and resilience.*

## Ultimate Skill:

**Aetherial Temporal Unveiling** - *Eldarion taps into the Aetherial Nexus, creating a temporal rift that allows him to observe and interact with specific moments from the past without altering the present. This advanced form of Chronicle Weaving enables Eldarion to access critical historical events, gather information, and even summon entities from different timelines to aid him in the current moment.*

## Equipment:

**Aetherial Archeologist's Attire:** Robes enchanted with Aetherial essence, enhancing Eldarion's magical abilities and providing protection.

**Chronoquill Staff:** A staff with Lumarian symbols, serving as a conduit for advanced Chronicle Weaving and elemental magic.

**Ethereal Lens:** A crystal lens that enhances Eldarion's perception of Aetherial energies, aiding in his studies and magical endeavors.

**Elemental Codex:** An ancient tome containing knowledge of Quad Elemental magic and advanced summoning rituals.

**Nexus Amulet:** An amulet infused with Aetherial Nexus essence, amplifying Eldarion's connection to the Aether and granting additional magical insight.

**Temporal Shroud:** A shimmering shroud that provides temporal protection, shielding Eldarion from potential temporal disturbances during his magical explorations.

**Aetherial Nexus Stone:** A crystalline stone acting as a focal point for Aetherial rituals, enhancing Eldarion's summoning abilities and empowering his Aetherial Nexus Mastery

# CHAPTER 18

# VEIL OF LUMINARY SHADOWS – PART 1

Evangeline Thorne, known across realms as The Alchemic Enchantress, moved gracefully through the corridors of Luminary. Her Charmed Garments swirled with ethereal hues as she made her way towards the alchemical chamber. A feeling of unease hung in the air, and Evangeline couldn't shake the sense that shadows concealed secrets waiting to be unravelled.

Her connection to Umbralis, the Luminary Alchemist, traced back to an encounter in the shadowed alleys of Luminary. Their paths had crossed, and the enigmatic Umbralis had recognized the alchemic potential within Evangeline. It was a connection that lingered in the background, a subtle dance of shadows that intertwined their fates.

Entering the alchemical chamber, Evangeline's eyes fell upon the alchemical apparatus. Umbral attire adorned the room like a shroud, a silent testament to Umbralis's presence. The alchemical elixirs she prepared seemed to hold a dual nature, a fusion of shadows and alchemy that resonated with Umbralis's Luminary Alchemy.

As Evangeline began her own alchemic brew, her thoughts drifted to the memory of her encounter with Umbralis. A clandestine meeting in the hidden corners of Luminary, where Umbralis had acknowledged the alchemic arts that flowed through Evangeline's veins. The Luminary Alchemist had hinted at a shared purpose, a weaving of destinies that transcended the boundaries of light and shadow.

Evangeline's enchanting aura radiated as she carefully mixed her potions, each concoction a testament to the harmony she sought to create. However, the shadows that clung to Umbralis's Luminary Alchemy were a stark contrast, a reminder that not all magic danced in the light.

As she worked, Evangeline sensed an undercurrent of deceit in the air. The shadows seemed to whisper secrets, and she wondered if Umbralis, with her allegiance hidden in the Luminary realm, held the key to unraveling the mysteries veiled in luminary shadows.

The connection between Umbralis and Master Voss remained a puzzle, a tapestry of luminary shadows woven with threads of intrigue. Evangeline felt a responsibility to navigate the delicate balance between her alchemic pursuits and the luminary shadows that sought to conceal the truth.

In the dim glow of the alchemical chamber, Evangeline continued her brew, weaving her own enchantments into the elixirs. The luminary shadows whispered, and as she glanced towards the Umbral attire, a subtle acknowledgment passed between her and Umbralis—a shared understanding that their paths were entwined, and the secrets of the luminary shadows were yet to unfold.

Evangeline's harrowing journey through the Voidshaper Sanctum took an ominous turn as she witnessed Umbralis in the throes of dark conjuration. The air crackled with suppressed energy as Umbralis meticulously drew and completed a foreboding circle. The atmosphere grew heavier with each stroke, and an unsettling tension gripped the void realm.

As the last line connected, a surge of ominous energy emanated from the completed circle. Shadows danced and coiled within, forming an ethereal gateway. In the heart of this abyssal vortex, a dark entity awaited its release.

Evangeline, caught between dread and fascination, observed Umbralis's measured movements. Her mentor, once a guiding figure in alchemical arts, now stood as a conjurer of shadows and architect of forbidden rituals. The circle pulsated with a malevolent energy that hinted at the unleashed entity's formidable power.

Suddenly, as Umbralis uttered incantations lost to the echoes of the void, the dark entity emerged. Its form, a manifestation of Umbralis's most intricate nightmares, twisted and contorted in the volatile magic of the void. Evangeline's senses recoiled at the sheer darkness that spilled forth, an entity unbound by the laws of Luminary.

The ritual's completion marked a shift in the void realm's fabric. The once dormant shadows now surged with newfound vigour, responding to the dark entity's presence. Umbralis, having achieved his arcane endeavors, locked eyes with Evangeline. In that shared gaze, she saw both triumph and a haunting sadness—a reflection of the sacrifices made to traverse the abyss between realms.

As the dark entity lingered in the void, Umbralis spoke to Evangeline through their telepathic link. He revealed the truth—that Luminary's demise was imminent, and her role as a reluctant consort held a crucial key to unraveling the shadows that enshrouded their realm.

Torn between loyalty and the weight of Luminary's fate, Evangeline steeled herself for the challenges ahead. The dark entity, now a silent spectator in the void, bore witness to the unfolding drama that would determine the destiny of Luminary and those entwined in the threads of shadowy magic.

But then, in a disorienting twist, darkness enveloped Evangeline's consciousness. The world blurred, and the last thing she saw before blacking out was Umbralis completing the ritual.

When she regained consciousness, a sense of disorientation clung to her. The Voidshaper Sanctum had transformed, and she found herself alone with Master Voss. Panic gripped her heart as she faced the looming figure draped in shadows.

Master Voss's words echoed through the void, revealing a twisted plan to erase Luminary's existence. The revelation of Luminary's imminent demise weighed heavily on Evangeline. The overwhelming responsibility thrust upon her shoulders and the prospect of becoming Master Voss's consort for the sake of hiding Luminary's truth filled her with dread.

In the unsettling discourse, a flicker of hope manifested through a relic bestowed upon her by Master Umbralis. The relic, a link to Umbralis through telepathy, suddenly connected. Relief washed over Evangeline as Umbralis's voice whispered into her mind, explaining the true situation. He had managed to evade Master Voss's clutches, saved by his vigilant familiar who sacrificed a fragment of itself to ensure Umbralis's escape.

In the void realm, where deception thrived, Umbralis's familiar remained undetected, a tiny beacon of connection bridging the gap between them. Evangeline clung to this lifeline, a silent understanding passing between her and Umbralis. Their alliance, born from shared secrets and the desire to unveil Luminary's fate, persisted despite the shadows seeking to envelop them.

As Master Voss continued his ominous plans, Evangeline concealed the knowledge bestowed upon her by Umbralis. She feigned compliance, all the while plotting with Umbralis through their telepathic link. The Luminary's demise and Master Voss's schemes had to be thwarted, and Evangeline, armed with alchemic arts and the silent support of Umbralis, prepared to navigate the treacherous currents of the void realm.

The Voidshaper Sanctum, a labyrinth of shadows and deceit, became the battleground for a clandestine war. Evangeline, now aware of the fragile existence of Luminary, embraced her role as a reluctant consort, her every action veiled in strategy. Together with Umbralis, they sought to protect Luminary's truth, unveiling the secrets that lingered in the luminary shadows and defying the machinations of the Voidshaper.

# CHAPTER 19

# VEIL OF LUMINARY SHADOWS – PART 2

In the present, as Aric's power grew and he became a proficient Voidwalker, his mastery over the void became unmistakably compatible with Master Voss. From the shadows, Evangeline, who posed as a consort while secretly serving as a spy for Umbralis, watched Aric in secret. The time had come for her to execute the plan that she and Master Umbralis had carefully crafted.

Aric's connection with the void had strengthened, and the intricate dance between void energies and his essence unfolded before Evangeline's watchful eyes. The plan devised by her and Master Umbralis was a delicate web of alchemic arts and enchantments, aiming to free Aric from the clutches of Master Voss.

Silently moving through the shadow-laden corridors of the Voidshaper Sanctum, Evangeline wove enchantments that concealed her presence from both Voidshapers and prying magical senses. Her alchemic senses tingled as she approached the focal point of Aric's void-wielding prowess.

As Aric delved deeper into the mysteries of the void under Master Voss's tutelage, he unknowingly walked a perilous path. The void, a realm of unpredictable energies and lurking shadows, threatened to consume him entirely. It was this vulnerability that Evangeline sought to exploit, guided by Umbralis's cryptic insights.

The plan unfolded as a symphony of alchemic nuances. Evangeline, with her Enchanting Phial in hand, carefully selected elixirs that would temporarily disrupt the alignment of Aric's void energies. These enchanted elixirs, when strategically administered, would create a fleeting dissonance in the harmony between Aric's essence and the void.

Moving closer to Aric's location, Evangeline detected the subtle ebb and flow of void energies around him. The Void minions, in their trance-like states, were oblivious to the impending intervention. With each step, she felt the weight of responsibility—to Aric, the unwitting vessel in this cosmic struggle.

As she neared the threshold of Aric's practice chamber, Evangeline carefully observed the rhythmic patterns of his void manipulation. The timing was crucial, and she synchronized her movements with the precise moment when Aric's connection with the void reached its zenith.

In a calculated motion, Evangeline unleashed the enchanted elixirs into the void-imbued atmosphere. The elixirs, a blend of alchemic wonders, diffused into the air like a shimmering mist. Aric, lost in the communion with the void, momentarily faltered as the harmonious resonance was disrupted.

Evangeline's heart raced as she witnessed the subtle effect of the elixirs taking hold. The disruption in Aric's connection, though temporary, created a window of opportunity. In that fleeting moment, a subtle signal was sent through the relic—a telepathic message to Umbralis.

" ," she projected her thoughts, "*The first phase of the plan is in motion. Aric's connection to the void has been momentarily disturbed. Now, guide me through the next steps. Luminary's fate hangs in the balance.*"

In the hidden recesses of the void, Umbralis received the message, and his plan, shrouded in ancient knowledge and alchemic mastery, began to unfurl. The intricate dance between light and shadow continued, and the destinies of Luminary, Aric, and the void itself stood at the crossroads of an unfolding cosmic drama.

The Voidshaper Sanctum stood silent, a tapestry of shadows and secrets veiled in the echoes of Aric's interrupted communion with the void. As Evangeline awaited Umbralis's guidance, the air quivered with anticipation of the next steps in their daring plan.

Umbralis's telepathic response resonated in Evangeline's mind, a spectral whisper that cut through the void's stillness. "*Evangeline, my faithful apprentice, you have done well. Now, as Aric grapples with the temporary disruption, we shall guide him to the brink where shadows and destiny intertwine."*

With the relic as their conduit and the subtle fragment of Umbralis's familiar maintaining the connection, Evangeline delved deeper into the void-woven corridors of the Sanctum. The plan, intricately designed to unravel the threads of Master Voss's influence, required precise timing and the seamless integration of alchemic arts and enchantments.

As Evangeline approached Aric, the luminary's expression betrayed a flicker of confusion, a momentary disruption in the seamless dance with the void. The enigmatic energies that surrounded him swirled, revealing the vulnerability that lay beneath his burgeoning power.

Umbralis's guidance echoed through the relic, *"Evangeline, now is the time to amplify the disruption. Use the Essence Infused Quill to inscribe an enchantment that resonates with the void's dissonance. Let the alchemic script weave through the fabric of the void, creating a subtle symphony that Aric's essence will follow."*

In response to Umbralis's directive, Evangeline retrieved the Essence Infused Quill—a tool that bridged the realms of alchemy and enchantment. With precise strokes, she inscribed an arcane script in the air, each stroke resonating with the disrupted void energies that lingered around Aric.

As the alchemic script took form, it emitted a subtle glow, weaving into the tapestry of shadows that enveloped Aric. The luminary, still attuned to the void but momentarily unsteady, became a canvas for the alchemic enchantment. The script resonated with the dissonance in the void, creating an ethereal harmony that guided Aric's essence along an altered path.

Evangeline's alchemic senses heightened as she witnessed the interplay between the disrupted void energies and the enchantment she had inscribed. The delicate balance between disruption and guidance unfolded, shaping Aric's connection in a way that defied Master Voss's dark intentions. Evangeline readied herself for the pivotal celestial alignment that would mark the climax of their plan. The whispers of the shadows echoed their approval, and the alchemic enchantress stood poised to steer Aric toward his true destiny. In the depths of the void, anticipation thrummed through the cosmic tapestry, waiting for the final, resounding chord of their cosmic dance.

Umbralis's voice echoed once more, *"Evangeline, the second phase is complete. Aric's essence now dances on the precipice of shadow and illumination. The final step is at hand. When the next celestial alignment occurs, channel your Charismatic Charms to enhance the enchantment. It shall be the catalyst for Aric's liberation."*

Evangeline nodded in silent acknowledgment, her resolve unwavering in the face of the cosmic ballet that unfolded. The Voidshaper Sanctum, witness to their clandestine efforts, held its secrets close, but Luminary's destiny teetered on the brink of revelation.

Evangeline tightened her grip on Aric's hand as they darted away from the watchful eye of the Voidshaper. "Aric, we mustn't linger here any longer," she urged, her voice a low murmur. "Master Voss will stop at nothing to reclaim you. We must find a way to break free from his grasp once and for all."

Aric nodded, his gaze hardened with resolve. "I understand, Evangeline. But where do we go from here? How do we escape his reach?"

Evangeline's eyes flickered with determination as she clasped Aric's hand. "We must seek refuge in the hidden places of Void Sectum, places where even Master Voss's influence cannot reach. There, we will find allies who will aid us in our quest to thwart his dark ambitions."

With a swift incantation, she shrouded them in an invisible veil, concealing their presence from any who might seek to thwart their escape. Together, they stole away from the throne room, the rush of freedom mingling with the weight of uncertainty that hung heavy in the air.

Meanwhile, in the depths of the sanctum, Master Voss's voice resonated with cold fury. "Find them," he commanded, his tone dripping with malice. "Bring the boy back to me, and ensure that the alchemist does not escape. They will not elude me for long. Their defiance will be met with the full force of my wrath."

As they fled from the looming threat, Evangeline's heart raced with a blend of relief and urgency. With Aric at her side, she navigated the twisting corridors, each turn bringing them closer to safety. Yet, amidst the chaos, her mind was consumed by thoughts of her master's familiar, concealed from prying eyes.

Finally, they arrived at the secret hiding place of the familiar, a secluded alcove tucked away from the chaos of the realm. Evangeline's eyes lit up as she beheld the shimmering presence of the hidden familiar, its essence pulsating with restrained power.

With determined strides, Evangeline approached the familiar's concealed form, her hand reaching out to touch the ethereal essence. As her fingers made contact, a surge of energy coursed through her, filling her with a sense of purpose and resolve.

With a whispered incantation, the fragment familiar channelled its latent magic, weaving the threads of teleportation to whisk Evangeline and Aric away from the looming shadows of the castle. In a flash of ethereal light, they found themselves standing in the cool darkness of a cavern, the oppressive presence of the Voidshaper's domain fading into the distance.

As they caught their breath, relief washed over them like a soothing tide. The cavern offered a temporary sanctuary, a respite from the chaos they had left behind. With weary smiles, Evangeline and Aric sank to the ground, their bodies weary from the exertion of their escape.

In the quiet solitude of the cave, they allowed themselves to rest, drawing strength from the tranquil embrace of the earth. The air was thick with the scent of damp stone and ancient magic, a reminder of the mysteries that lay hidden within the depths of the earth.

As they rested and regained their strength, their minds turned to the challenges that lay ahead. But for now, they basked in the newfound freedom of the cavern, grateful for the chance to gather their thoughts and prepare for the journey that awaited them.

After their short rest, Evangeline felt the familiar tug of Umbralis's presence in her mind. With a deep breath, she focused her thoughts, reaching out to the shadowy entity that had guided her through countless trials.

"*Master Umbralis*," she called silently, her mental voice echoing in the depths of her consciousness. "*We have escaped the castle. Aric and I are safe for now.*"

A ripple of shadows danced across her mind, a silent acknowledgment from her enigmatic mentor. Evangeline felt a surge of gratitude at the reassurance, knowing that Umbralis was watching over them, even from afar.

"*We are in a cavern outside the Voidshaper's domain*," she continued, relaying their whereabouts to Umbralis. "*It seems we have found a temporary sanctuary, but we must remain vigilant.*"

As she conveyed their situation to Umbralis, Evangeline couldn't shake the feeling of unease that lingered in the back of her mind. The shadows whispered of dangers yet to come, urging her to stay alert and prepared for whatever challenges lay ahead.

With her report delivered, Evangeline settled into a watchful vigil, her senses attuned to the subtle shifts in the shadows around them. As long as Umbralis remained by their side, she knew they would find a way to overcome whatever trials awaited them.

# CHAPTER 20

# THREADS OF DESTINY

As the celestial alignment approached, casting an otherworldly glow upon the cavern where Evangeline and Aric sought refuge, a veil of shadows began to unfurl. Unbeknownst to them, a clandestine force stirred in the depths of Luminary—a force that would introduce an unforeseen twist to their journey. In the heart of the cavern, where shadows danced in the dim light, a figure emerged from the depths of darkness.

This enigmatic being, draped in a cloak of ethereal shadows, navigated the void with an eerie grace. Its presence sent ripples through the fabric of reality, whispering secrets to the shadows that clung to the walls. This mysterious entity, known as the Umbral Arbiter, had long observed the struggles of Evangeline and Aric as they faced the machinations of Master Voss.

The Umbral Arbiter was no ally of Luminary or Eldermere but a guardian of the cosmic balance—an entity born from the convergence of primal shadows and cosmic energies.

The Umbral Arbiter's motives remained shrouded in ambiguity as it moved through the cavern with an air of detached neutrality, its form ever-shifting like the shadows it commanded.

Observing Aric's journey and Evangeline's interventions, the cosmic scales tipped in an unforeseen direction. In a spectral whisper that resonated through the void, the Umbral Arbiter addressed Evangeline, "Alchemic Enchantress, your efforts have not gone unnoticed.

The celestial alignment approaches, and the destiny of Luminary hangs in the balance. Yet, there are forces at play beyond even your alchemic senses." Evangeline, taken aback by the sudden appearance of the Umbral Arbiter, questioned its intent.

"Who are you, and what part do you play in this cosmic drama?" The Umbral Arbiter's response was enigmatic,

"I am the Veilwalker, the arbiter of shadows. Luminary's fate is entwined with the cosmic threads, and I am here to ensure that the balance is maintained. However, the shadows whisper of an impending disruption, a force that transcends the designs of both Master Voss and Umbralis."

As the Umbral Arbiter's revelation hung in the air, the Voidshaper Sanctum resonated with an uncanny stillness. The celestial alignment drew near, and the cosmic forces converged, setting the stage for a revelation that would reshape the destiny of Luminary.

Unknown to all, an ancient *prophecy*, obscured by the veils of time, hinted at a choice that would determine the realm's ultimate fate. The Veilwalker, a cosmic guardian unbound by allegiance, prepared to unveil the threads of destiny and guide Luminary toward a path only glimpsed in the echoes of shadowy *prophecy*.

The cosmic dance of light and shadow unfolded, and as the celestial alignment painted the sanctum in hues of mystic radiance, the Veilwalker's presence became a harbinger of unforeseen twists and revelations. Luminary, teetering on the edge of destiny, awaited the revelation that would pierce the veil of shadows and illuminate the path toward an uncertain future.

As the celestial alignment reached its zenith, casting an ethereal glow upon the Voidshaper Sanctum, Luminary, the realm of intricate magic, stood at the crossroads of destiny, unaware of the cosmic threads converging upon it. As the Veilwalker's presence resonated in the sanctum, the threads of fate began to weave a tapestry of revelation.

In the heart of the cosmic convergence, Aric, now a formidable Voidwalker, stood as the focal point of both Master Voss's ambitions and the cryptic designs of Umbralis. His connection with the void had grown exponentially, drawing upon the celestial energies that bathed the sanctum in celestial radiance.

Evangeline, the Alchemic Enchantress, observed Aric with a mix of anticipation and concern. The Umbral Arbiter, Veilwalker of shadows, hovered in the periphery, its form ever-shifting like the cosmic energies that surrounded it.

In a whisper that echoed through the void, the Veilwalker addressed Evangeline, "The threads of destiny are woven with delicate precision, and Luminary stands at the nexus of cosmic forces. The choices made in this celestial alignment will resonate through the fabric of time."

Evangeline, her alchemic senses heightened by the cosmic energies, sought guidance from the enigmatic being. "What must we do to navigate these threads of destiny? How can we ensure the balance is maintained?"

The Veilwalker's response carried an air of cosmic wisdom, "The cosmic balance is a delicate dance between light and shadow. Aric's journey is intricately tied to Luminary's fate, but there exists a choice that transcends the designs of both Master Voss and Umbralis. It is a choice only Aric can make, and the echoes of that decision will reverberate through the realms."

As the celestial energies intensified, Aric felt a profound resonance within himself. The void within him whispered secrets, and the cosmic threads entwined around him as if awaiting a decision that would shape the destiny of Luminary.

Evangeline, empowered by alchemic arts and guided by the Veilwalker's revelations, approached Aric. "Aric, the threads of destiny are in your hands. There is a choice before you, one that transcends the influences of those who seek to manipulate. Listen to the whispers of the void within, and let your heart guide the path you choose."

Aric, torn between the cosmic forces that sought to shape him, felt the weight of the impending decision. The celestial alignment reached its peak, and the sanctum resonated with an otherworldly harmony.

In that pivotal moment, Aric closed his eyes, attuning himself to the cosmic energies and the echoes of the void. The whispers within him became a chorus of possibilities, each thread of destiny vying for prominence.

As Luminary held its breath, the Veilwalker's form shifted, and the cosmic tapestry quivered with anticipation. The threads of destiny awaited Aric's choice, a choice that would echo through the realms and determine the course of Luminary's existence.

The celestial resonance lingered in the sanctum, and Aric, the Voidwalker, stood at the nexus of cosmic forces. The threads of destiny entwined around him, whispering secrets only he could decipher. The echoes of the void resonated within his very being, unlocking the full potential of his newfound class.

Aric's Umbral Scepter pulsated with power, resonating with the duality of his elemental affinities—Void and the surprising Essence of the Dead. The Shadowsoul Raiment clad him in ethereal armor, a manifestation of his connection to shadows and the departed souls that now echoed within him.

As Luminary held its breath, Aric's mind became a canvas for the cosmic forces at play. His Voidshaping abilities, honed through rigorous training, now expanded into an untapped potential—Shadow Army Conjuring. The shadows responded to his command, materializing into an army of ephemeral entities. They shifted and morphed at his will, guardians and attackers drawn from the depths of the void.

With a thought, Aric summoned those— silhouettes and ethereal beasts that moved in sync with his desires. The Shadowsoul Raiment flickered, resonating with the dance of shadows, and the sanctum became an ever-shifting battleground where the line between reality and the void blurred.

The Shadow Army Conjuring added a layer of versatility to Aric's arsenal. He felt the ebb and flow of shadows, their whispers guiding his strategic maneuvers. Eclipse Grasp, one of his active skills, became a symphony of shadow tendrils ensnaring and immobilizing foes, creating openings for the shadow entities to assail.

Yet, the revelation didn't stop there. A surprising twist unfurled—the dormant Essence of the Dead within Aric stirred. This secondary element, embracing both Light and Shadow aspects, unlocked a broader spectrum of abilities. The Umbral Scepter, now a conduit for both Void and Essence of the Dead, resonated with the harmonious balance within Aric.

His Umbral Scepter bathed in illuminating energy, Aric channelled the pure essence of departed souls. The Light aspect granted him the ability to heal and dispel darkness, bringing an unexpected layer to his repertoire. Abyssal Veil, another of his active skills, now shrouded him in an ethereal veil that rendered him temporarily intangible and immune to physical attacks.

As Aric navigated the delicate interplay between light and shadow, Luminary witnessed a Voidwalker who had transcended expectations. The sanctum echoed with the clash of shadows and the radiant hum of ethereal energy.

In the quiet moments between battles, Aric pondered the significance of his choices. The Veilwalker, ever-watchful, whispered cosmic truths. The threads of destiny, once elusive, now responded to his command. The sanctum became a proving ground for Aric's decision-making skills, each strategic move a testament to his mastery over the cosmic forces that enveloped Luminary.

As the cosmic resonance faded, leaving Luminary in a state of anticipation, Aric, the Voidwalker, stood ready for the challenges that awaited. The shadows and light, once opposing forces, now coalesced in a harmonious dance under his command. The echoes of the void lingered, hinting at the unforeseen challenges and revelations that lay ahead on his magical odyssey.

In the cavern where the three of them sought refuge, Evangeline stood at the ready, her senses attuned to the subtle whispers of the shadows. With unwavering patience, she awaited her master's command, knowing that their next move would be crucial in the unfolding cosmic drama. As the celestial energies ebbed and flowed around them, Evangeline's resolve remained steadfast, her alchemic senses poised to decipher the cryptic threads of fate that bound them all.

# CHAPTER 21

# THE DECAGON SHADOW COURT'S CONCLAVE

In the aftermath of Aric's daring escape from Master Voss's clutches, the sanctum trembled with a palpable sense of unrest. Master Voss, his fury unchecked by Aric's elusiveness, swore to reclaim his prized vessel by any means necessary. The shadows, unsettled by the disruption to their carefully laid plans, hissed with the promise of vengeance and retribution, casting a foreboding shadow over the once-hallowed grounds.

Master Voss, clad in the shadowy remnants of his former self, summoned the Decagon Shadowcourt—his ten faithful generals of the void. Although not fully manifested, the power of the Decagon Shadowcourt was formidable. They materialized in the dim-lit sanctum, their forms coalescing from the very shadows that clung to the walls.

Master Voss's weapon became his temporary vessel. The remnants of his essence intertwined with the dark energies emanating from the weapon, allowing him to command his loyal generals. The weapon, a conduit for Voss's authority, pulsed with otherworldly power.

Master Voss singled out one of the generals, a shadowy figure known as Zephyra, a mistress of illusions and the art of subterfuge. "Zephyra!" Master Voss intoned, "Summon the Decagon Shadowcourt. We have a task at hand, and our plans must not be thwarted by the interference of the Luminary and his meddling consort."

Zephyra, a silhouette with ethereal grace, bowed gracefully before Master Voss. "As you command, Master Voss."

In the heart of the sanctum, Zephyra began the summoning ritual. The shadows danced and twisted, forming a gateway through which the remaining nine generals of the Decagon Shadowcourt emerged. Each general bore a unique aspect of void magic, a testament to their mastery over the cosmic forces.

Master Voss, his gaze penetrating the veil between realms, addressed his generals. "Our plans for Aric's ascension must not be delayed. The Luminary and his apprentice pose a threat that cannot be ignored. I have chosen you, my most loyal Shadowcourt, to ensure the success of our endeavors."

The generals, shrouded in shadows, listened intently to their master's commands. Their loyalty to Master Voss was unwavering, and their existence was bound to the fulfillment of his dark ambitions.

"Seek out a temporary vessel for my essence," Master Voss instructed. "Once secured, resume the ritual. Aric must be reclaimed, and the shadows will bow to my dominion."

The generals dispersed into the void, leaving the sanctum in an eerie silence. Master Voss, now confined to the temporary vessel, contemplated the threads of destiny that intertwined with Luminary and Aric. The Decagon Shadowcourt, dispersed across realms, set in motion the next phase of their malevolent design.

The sanctum, a nexus of shadows and deceit, awaited the unfolding of the void's machinations. The Decagon Shadowcourt, guided by the will of their master, embarked on a clandestine mission to secure a vessel and resume the ritual that would plunge Luminary into darkness.

Master Voss's voice echoed through the darkness, his words laced with malice and determination. "Let the shadows converge, and darkness reign once more."

In the dim-lit corridors of the sanctum, the shadows stirred, obeying Master Voss's command with a sinister obedience. They coiled and writhed, forming a malevolent shroud that enveloped the throne room, casting it into deeper darkness.

Meanwhile, Master Voss's minions continued their relentless search throughout the labyrinthine passages of the sanctum, their eyes scanning every shadow, every corner, in pursuit of Aric and Evangeline. Unbeknownst to them, their quarry had already slipped through their grasp, leaving behind no trace of their escape.

As the tension thickened in the air, the minions pressed on with renewed determination, unaware that their efforts were in vain. The shadows seemed to mock their fruitless search, whispering secrets that eluded their grasp.

But amidst the encroaching darkness, a glimmer of hope flickered—a beacon of light amidst the shadows. Aric and Evangeline, determined to defy Master Voss's tyranny, pressed onward, their resolve unyielding.

With each step they took, they drew closer to freedom, closer to the allies who awaited them in the hidden recesses of Luminary. And though the path ahead was fraught with peril, they knew that together, they would face whatever darkness lay in wait.

For in the heart of the void, where shadows danced and secrets whispered, the light of courage and defiance shone brightest, illuminating the path to redemption and liberation.

# CHAPTER 22

# CHRONICLES OF ELEMENTAL HARMONY: THE SHATTERED PROPHECY

### Celestial Revelations:

Returning to the moment when Master Elowen and his companions delved into the depths of *prophecy*, the air crackled with anticipation. Lirael, Kaelin, Master Elowen, and Eldarion stood before the ancient glyphs, their eyes alight with determination as they sought to unravel the mysteries veiled within.

Eldarion, the Archeologist, stood within the sanctum of ancient knowledge, surrounded by artifacts and relics that whispered tales of bygone eras. His eyes, deep pools of cosmic wisdom, gleamed with the echoes of countless journeys through the Aetherial Nexus.

### Advanced Chronicle Weaving:

Eldarion extended his hands, fingers tracing invisible patterns in the air. The chamber shimmered as illusions unfolded, each thread of time meticulously woven into a tapestry of historical events. His advanced Chronicle Weaving skill allowed him to navigate the annals of time with unparalleled precision.

As the illusions settled, revealing scenes from the past, Eldarion began to speak. "In the tapestry of cosmic events, a *prophecy* of great import emerges. Listen, for the echoes of destiny resonate through the very fabric of reality."

## The *Prophecy* of the Returning Void Shaper:

*"In twilight's grasp, where shadows weave,*

*Mysterious whispers, in the night they conceive.*

*Cosmic tapestry, a tale of void's return,*

*Guided by unseen hands, their secrets to discern."*

Eldarion's voice, a harmonic blend of past and present, carried the weight of prophecies yet to unfold. The chamber flickered with astral energies as the *prophecy* continued to unravel.

## Glyphs of Power, Ancient Lore Inscribed:

*"Glyphs of power, ancient lore inscribed,*

*Veiled identities stir, in cosmic lore described.*

*Their gaze upon the prophecy falls,*

*Threads of destiny bind, as enigmatic echoes call."*

The Aetherial Nexus responded to Eldarion's command, projecting glyphs that danced in ethereal patterns. The gathered scholars and seekers watched in awe as the *prophecy's* glyphs took on a life of their own.

## Celestial Parchment, Where Destinies Align:

*"Celestial parchment, where destinies align,*

*One in shadows deciphers, in the mystic's shrine.*

*Their awakening, an astral dance in flight,*

*Wisdom guiding realms through the veiled night."*

Eldarion's hands moved with grace, conjuring images of celestial realms and mystical shrines. The *prophecy's* verses echoed through the chamber, resonating with the unseen forces that shaped the destiny of realms.

## Key to the Celestial Gate:

*"Key to the celestial gate, in shadows they wait,*

*Intricate fate unfolds, destiny's mysterious dictate.*

*Stars in eventide witness the cosmic art,*

*As unseen hands guide, realms never to part."*

As the final verses of the celestial *prophecy* hung in the air like a cosmic decree, Eldarion, his gaze solemn, turned his attention to the enigmatic figure of the ancient Oracle from Lumaria. Unseen by Kaelin and the others, the Oracle stood among the assembly, her presence imbued with a weighty significance that hinted at untold secrets and hidden truths.

## Introduction of Celestria, the Ancient Oracle from Luminara:

*"In this cosmic dance, where prophecies intertwine,*

*Celestria, the Oracle, brings wisdom divine.*

*From Luminara's embrace, her presence unfolds,*

*As Eldarion's hands the prophecy holds."*

Celestria, veiled in the radiance of celestial energies, stepped forward. Her eyes, luminous with the wisdom of epochs, met Eldarion's with a shared understanding of the cosmic forces at play. Though unseen by Kaelin and the others, Eldarion alone perceived her presence, recognizing the weighty significance she carried within the chamber.

*"As Eldarion has unveiled the prophecy's call,*

*Luminara's secrets, together we shall enthrall.*

*The celestial gate awaits, the void shaper's fate,*

*In unity, our destinies resonate."*

As Eldarion and Celestria stood united, the cosmic currents swirled around them, marking the beginning of a celestial alliance that would shape the destinies of realms and unveil the truths hidden within the cosmic tapestry.

The chamber embraced a hushed anticipation as Eldarion and Celestria, their energies entwined, prepared to delve further into the cosmic secrets revealed by the *prophecy*.

## Astral Nexus Unveiled:

*"Through Luminara's astral embrace,*

*Veils of secrets, we shall chase.*

*The Aetherial Nexus, our guide and gate,*

*To fathom the echoes of the cosmic debate."*

As Eldarion uttered these words, the Aetherial Nexus pulsed with renewed vigor. Its ethereal glow intensified, casting a celestial radiance that bathed the assembly in otherworldly luminescence.

## Unified Sight into the Tapestry:

*"Eldarion's mastery, Celestria's lore,*

*Unified sight into the tapestry we implore.*

*Glyphs and echoes, threads of fate,*

*In this celestial union, our destinies equate."*

Eldarion and Celestria, their eyes reflecting the luminescent glow of the Aetherial Nexus, focused their collective energies on the cosmic tapestry. Scenes unfolded, revealing ancient alliances, cosmic battles, and the enigmatic dance of the Void Shaper through the annals of time.

## The Triumvirate's Decree:

*"With ancient relics united, a triumvirate's decree,*

*In Twilight's union, their powers fuse in harmony.*

*Arcane artifacts entwine, a key to the void's demise,*

*Combined forces of magic-users, where the void shaper lies."*

The vision shifted to depict the union of arcane artifacts held by each magic user – Kaelin, Lirael, and an unseen third figure yet to be revealed. The convergence of their powers formed a celestial key, a weapon against the impending threat of the Returning Void Shaper.

## The Unseen Third:

*"An unseen third, in shadows concealed,*

*Their destiny intertwined, the cosmic battlefield.*

*In realms uncharted, their power surges,*

*A guardian unseen as the prophecy urges."*

As the verses echoed, the assembled crowd exchanged curious glances. The identity of the third figure remained veiled, adding an air of mystery to the unfolding cosmic drama.

## The Prophecy's Charge:

*"The Prophecy charges our cosmic stride,*

*In unity, secrets and destinies coincide.*

*Eldarion and Celestria, cosmic conduits,*

*Guided by fate, unveiling truths in celestial pursuits."*

Eldarion and Celestria, attuned to the cosmic currents, exchanged a knowing glance. Their journey into the realms of *prophecy* had only just begun, and the threads of destiny awaited their skilled hands to weave a path through the celestial tapestry.

As the luminous energy of the Aetherial Nexus settled, the chamber retained a lingering glow – a testament to the revelations unveiled and the cosmic union forged by Eldarion, the Archeologist, and Celestria, the Ancient Oracle from Luminara.

Celestria, with a serene smile, acknowledged the significance of the newly revealed verse. "In the cosmic dance of fate, Eldarion, the Triumvirate shall be the architects of a new chapter, guided by the cosmic design that unfolds with each step."

As Eldarion and Celestria gazed into the Aetherial Nexus, the unspoken verse echoed through the chamber, setting the stage for the Triumvirate's journey into the uncharted territories of the cosmic tapestry.

As Eldarion concluded the intricate weaving of the cosmic tapestry, beads of perspiration adorned his forehead, and his breaths came in labored gasps. The toll of unraveling the profound *prophecy* through his advanced chronicle-weaving skills left him on the brink of exhaustion. Swiftly, Master Elowen and Kaelin rushed forward, catching Eldarion before he could succumb to the weariness that enveloped him. Gratitude emanated from their expressions as they acknowledged Eldarion's invaluable contribution in deciphering the *prophecy*, the weight of destiny resting upon their shoulders.

In the aftermath of his exertion, Eldarion found solace in the hushed background, lying in silence as he rested upon the cool surface. With beads of perspiration clinging to his forehead, he closed his eyes, allowing the rhythmic sound of his breath to accompany the subtle whispers of the cosmic energies. The room echoed with the weighty gratitude expressed by Master Elowen and Kaelin, a testament to the significance of the deciphered *prophecy*. Eldarion, though physically spent, embraced the tranquility that enveloped him, regaining his composure and replenishing the energy that had been expended in the unraveling of the intricate threads of fate.

# CHAPTER 23

# ELDERMERE'S LEGACY AND LUMINAL'S ECHO

Master Elowen stood at the outside the balcony of the archive, looking down at the city that had risen from the ashes of Luminara. The sun cast its warm glow on the rebuilt structures, but the echoes of Luminal's grandeur lingered in Master Elowen's thoughts.

As he gazed upon Eldermere's spires, Kaelin and Lirael approached, their curiosity etched across their faces. The air hummed with unspoken questions.

"Master, before we embark on our next journey," Lirael began, "I am curious. All my life, I have known this place as Eldermere. The Elemental Spirits shared fragments of its history with me, but I still struggle to connect the dots. Why does Eldermere hold a connection to Luminara? And where is Luminara, truly?"

Master Elowen's eyes reflected the weight of memories. He gestured for them to sit by the Elemental Nexus, where the energies of all four elements converged.

"Eldermere," he began, "was reborn from the ruins of Luminara, an ancient city that stood as a beacon of Lumarian knowledge for countless ages. Luminara wasn't just a city; it was a repository of wisdom, a sanctuary where scholars delved into the secrets of the elements."

As Master Elowen spoke, the images of Luminara's majestic architecture and towering libraries came alive in his words. The tales of Luminara's significance unfolded, painting a vivid picture for Kaelin and Lirael.

"During the Voidshaper's invasion, Luminara faced its darkest hour. We managed to salvage some of its essence, the Lumarian knowledge, and carry it forward to Eldermere. The decision to rename the city was a tribute to

Luminara's legacy, a promise to preserve its teachings despite the physical loss."

Kaelin's eyes reflected a mix of understanding and curiosity. "But Master, why did Luminara hold such importance? What secrets were hidden within its walls?"

Master Elowen leaned forward, his eyes fixed on the Elemental Nexus. "Luminara wasn't merely a city; it was a convergence of ancient prophecies, elemental wisdom, and the very essence of the Elemental Harmony. It housed the Lumarian Consortium, an assembly of scholars dedicated to understanding the intricacies of our world."

As the trio sat by the Nexus, the Elemental Spirits seemed to whisper tales of Luminara's profound connection to the Elemental Harmony, its role in prophecies that shaped destinies, and the mysteries that still awaited unraveling.

Lirael, her curiosity piqued, asked, "So, Master, as we venture into the unknown, are we also unraveling the secrets of Luminara and the ancient prophecies?"

Master Elowen nodded, a gleam of determination in his eyes. "Indeed. Luminara's legacy lives on within Eldermere, and as we seek the truth about the Voidshaper, we may uncover the threads that tie our present struggles to Luminara's ageless wisdom."

The Elemental Nexus pulsed with a harmonious energy, resonating with the journey that awaited them and the mysteries yet to be unveiled.

As they reach their separate room in the dimly lit chamber of the Lumarian Consortium, Master Elowen's gaze drifted into the past, a brief yet poignant flashback materializing before his eyes. The air seemed to shimmer with the echoes of a pivotal moment—the unanimous decision to rename their once-vulnerable city Luminara to Eldermere. The consortium, a collective of magic-users and scholars, had gathered in unity, their intentions clear and resolute.

As the flashback dissipated, Master Elowen addressed the assembled Lumarian Consortium, his voice carrying the weight of history and the promise of a resilient future. "Luminaries, we stand on the precipice of transformation. Eldermere is not just a name change; it is a beacon of hope, a symbol of our perseverance in the face of adversity. Let this renaming resonate within our very essence, forging a path towards a destiny shaped by Lumarian strength." said Magnetra The Polarity Nexuscommander of the Lumarian Consortium

The words lingered in the air, the consortium absorbing the significance of their collective decision.

## *Start of Flashback:*

As the Lumarian Consortium deliberated their next steps, a solemn voice resonated in the chamber. Magnetra acted like a true commander in front of the members, she understood the weight of the decision. "Elowen, this is my last order, I order you... no, as a fellow Lumarian, we are requesting you to stay here in Eldermere. Protect our legacy, uphold our teachings, and prevent the loss of the wisdom we have safeguarded through the ages."

In response to the looming sense of disbandment, a Lumarian consort member, Luminos, stepped forward with a determined expression. "Do not fret; this disbandment is only temporary. One day, we will reunite under the same roof once more," she assured the consortium, injecting a note of optimism into the heavy air. "There is something fishy about all of this, and we need to find a solution. Everyone, come, and leave something that can be used as a communication device. Each member, put your magic and heart into leaving your essence. When the time has come for us to reunite, we will have the ability to do so."

The Lumarians nodded in understanding, recognizing the importance of maintaining a connection even in their physical separation. They approached one by one, leaving behind tokens infused with their essence—a collective promise to reunite when the cosmic forces aligned. The chamber echoed with the hum of magic and the resonance of Lumarian determination, setting the stage for a future reunion that would defy the constraints of time and space.

Master Elowen pondered the events of the final exchange and noticed a conspicuous absence. *"No, it can't be Umbralis - The Umbral Alchemist,"* he mused silently. Umbralis, with his peculiar yet endearing demeanor, had not been present during that critical moment. A sense of suspicion crept into Elowen's thoughts, but he chose to keep it to himself for the time being. He recalled fond memories shared with Umbralis, acknowledging him as a good ally, albeit a bit eccentric. Elowen harbored a desire to uncover the truth, yet with Eldarion still in recovery, he found himself compelled to bide his time and await the opportune moment to address the mystery surrounding Umbralis's absence.

The next five years unfolded with the rebirth of Luminara as Eldermere, and during this period, Elowen received an unexpected artifact message from his friendly rival, Elyndor Wayan - The Ethereal Enclave. The message conveyed a desire to meet in person, and without hesitation, Elowen teleported to their usual dueling ground. "Hey there, you loner. You look as gloomy as ever," teased Elyndor as Elowen retaliated with water and wind magic, freezing and then unfreezing him. The banter continued under the starry night and moonlight, and Elyndor shared his experiences, reminiscing about the good old days. Amid the heartfelt conversations, Elyndor couldn't resist injecting humor into the reunion. As he showed the engagement ring, Elowen, taken aback, instinctively smacked him on the head. The revelation unfolded that Elyndor had become engaged to Avonlea Aquafin - The Aqueous Enchantress. Amidst laughter and teasing, the banter continued, with Elowen sulkily questioning when this had happened. Elyndor, not missing a beat, cheekily responded with a mischievous grin, "Last month, under the stars and a full moon."

In response, Elowen, feigning annoyance, conjured water and wind magic, freezing Elyndor momentarily again before thawing him out. Amidst laughter, Elyndor, now warmer, continued his tale. As the laughter and teasing continued, Elyndor wrapped up his humorous tale with a smirk. "And here we thought you were gay," Elowen teased, prompting more laughter between the friends. Elyndor, with a puzzled expression, inquired about the source of this assumption. Elowen, with a playful glint in his eye, not wanting to reveal his friend simply responded with, "Yo mama."

This unexpected twist elicited a burst of laughter from both Elyndor and Elowen, their camaraderie shining through amid the banter. The banter, humor, and warmth of their reunion captured the essence of their enduring friendship, solidified through years of shared adventures and playful jests.

The light-hearted banter added a touch of comedy to the otherwise serious exchange, highlighting the enduring camaraderie between the old friends. Elyndor shared the story of their journey and exploration, uncovering a ruin with inscriptions related to the spirits of the elements. A year later, Elyndor and Avonlea now known as the Wayfin visited Elowen again, this time with a baby boy named Kaelin. Expressing concerns for their child's safety during further exploration, they entrusted Kaelin to Elowen's care. Avonlea enchanted Baby Kaelin with the ability to awaken his powers at the age of 7 and bestowed a protective enchantment for his safety.

Two years after the Wayfins entrusted their son Kaelin to Elowen's care, a mysterious basket arrived at Master Elowen's doorstep. Contained within was a baby girl with sparkling eyes, and four carefully selected items. The first was a letter addressed to Elowen, bearing the seal of the Luminary Consortium. The missive explained the necessity of having a guardian for their child and expressed the deep trust they had in Elowen's abilities.

Beside the letter lay three significant items. The first was an intricately crafted staff, resonating with latent magical energies. The second, a pocket watch, contained the essence and memories of Lirael's parents, allowing her to connect with her roots. The final item was a sealed letter, meant for Lirael to open on her sixteenth birthday.

Elowen, filled with both surprise and gratitude, marveled at the unexpected responsibility bestowed upon him. With the Luminary Consortium's implicit trust, he pledged to protect and guide both Kaelin and the newly arrived baby girl, whom they named Lirael.

As the years passed, Elowen watched over the children, nurturing their potential. Kaelin, under the enchantment cast by Avonlea, gradually awakened his powers. Meanwhile, Lirael, unaware of the secrets embedded in the pocket watch and sealed letter, grew into a spirited and curious young girl.

### *End of Flashback:*

Under the dappled sunlight filtering through the leaves, Kaelin and Lirael engaged in their weekly sparring session in the familiar training area. The open space, surrounded by towering trees, created an idyllic yet challenging environment. The ground beneath them was soft, covered with a carpet of fallen leaves, and the air was filled with the gentle rustle of foliage.

Water sources, both small streams and crystal-clear ponds, were strategically scattered throughout the sparring ground. The presence of water added an extra layer of complexity to their training, requiring them to adapt to the ever-changing terrain.

Amidst the ethereal dance of magic, Kaelin and Lirael, the two components of the Triumvirate, engaged in a captivating exchange of power. The air crackled with anticipation as Kaelin conjured a high-pressure water lance using the water source around him, propelling it towards Lirael with the precision of a seasoned mage. The lance, shimmering with liquid energy, cut through the air with a mesmerizing azure glow.

Lirael's response was swift and graceful. With fluid movements, she erected a shimmering barrier that intercepted the water lance. The barrier emitted a melodic hum, resonating with the potency of her magical defense. Simultaneously, mirages danced around the training ground, an illusionary display that left even Kaelin momentarily entranced.

As the magical ballet continued, Kaelin marveled at the symphony of colors. The water lance, a cascade of azure brilliance, clashed with the barrier's radiant energy, creating an ephemeral display of vibrant hues. Lirael, in her elemental prowess, harnessed fire and wind, blending them into a fiery vortex that crackled with the warmth of an enchanted blaze. The gust of wind added a tangible force to the spectacle, stirring the surroundings in tandem with the magical elements.

Transitioning from defense to offense, Kaelin soared into the air with the grace of a winged mage. His Aquaforge Blade, pointed downward, unleashed a torrential descent of pressurized water droplets. Each droplet gleamed with liquid energy, forming a cascade that sparkled like a crystalline waterfall. In response, Lirael maneuvered through the aerial onslaught with agile precision, her every movement an elegant choreography against the canvas of the blue sky.

Grounded but undeterred, Lirael called upon the earth beneath her. The ground responded with a resonant hum as a rising pillar elevated her further into the battleground. Flames erupted from her fingertips, merging seamlessly with the earth element. The resulting cascade of blazing elements provided a formidable defense against Kaelin's aquatic barrage. The training ground, once a serene space, transformed into a canvas where the Triumvirate painted the tapestry of their growing powers.

Caught during this elemental exchange, Kaelin demonstrated his mastery with a mist clone, a phantom projection that dodged seamlessly. The real Kaelin remained untouched, poised to continue the intricate magical ballet in their mid-air duel. The symphony of elements unfolded, captivating any spectator with its sheer beauty and power.

As the scene transitioned, Lirael seized the initiative, unleashing a tri-elemental barrage towards Kaelin. The intensity of her magical onslaught caught Kaelin off guard, and he found himself hurtling towards the ocean. In a display of quick thinking, he conjured a protective water shield, cushioning the impact and preventing himself from submerging into the depths below.

Emerging from the water, Kaelin, though visibly shaken, summoned his Aquaforge Blade once again. Rising from the ocean with a determined spirit, he conjured a massive tidal wave, a testament to his control over water. Unfazed by the approaching aquatic force, Lirael readied herself, channeling her tri-elemental prowess to unleash a counterblast with equal intensity.

The clash of elements reached a crescendo, creating a visual spectacle of magical energies colliding. The training ground transformed into a battleground of opposing forces, waves and blasts echoing the evolving capabilities of the Triumvirate. The elemental symphony continued a vivid demonstration of the Triumvirate's mastery over their newfound powers.

Exhausted and exhilarated, Kaelin and Lirael acknowledged the end of their intense training session with a silent agreement. Collapsing onto the ground, chests rising and falling in tandem, the echoes of their magical exertions lingered in the air. The training ground, now a sanctum of accomplishment, bore witness to their trials and triumphs.

In the quiet aftermath, Kaelin, still catching his breath, couldn't help but express his admiration for Lirael's prowess. "Lirael, that was truly impressive! The way you danced through the battlefield, seamlessly changing elements—it was mesmerizing to see. Your control over fire, earth, and wind is unparalleled." His words, were a genuine testament to the awe he felt.

Lirael, reciprocating the appreciation, smiled, her eyes reflecting the satisfaction of their growth. "And your water-based attacks were incredible, Kaelin. That tidal wave maneuver, especially after taking a hit, was both defensive and strategic. Your quick thinking amid our magical exchange is a testament to your adaptability and resourcefulness." Her words echoed with genuine admiration.

As they shared mutual appreciation, a sense of camaraderie deepened between Kaelin and Lirael. The echoes of their elemental clash now resonated with the harmony of newfound respect and understanding. The training ground, witness to their trials and triumphs, became a space where the Triumvirate not only honed their powers but forged bonds that would withstand the cosmic challenges awaiting them.

# CHAPTER 24

# THE SAGE'S OBSERVANCE

As the echoes of the elemental clash between Kaelin and Lirael resonated through the magical realm, Master Elowen, attuned to the currents of power, felt the pulsating waves of energy. Intrigued by the intensity of the magical exchange, he decided to venture to the training grounds where the Triumvirate had honed their newfound abilities.

Upon reaching the training grounds, Elowen concealed his presence, observing the aftermath of the magical spectacle. The air still crackled with the remnants of elemental energy, and the training ground bore witness to the display of the Triumvirate's growing powers.

Amid the magical aftermath, Kaelin and Lirael, chests still heaving from the exertion, caught their breath. Sensing their mentor's presence, they exchanged glances and nodded in silent acknowledgment.

Master Elowen emerged from the shadows, his expression a mixture of amazement and pride. "Impressive," he remarked, his voice carrying the weight of wisdom. "The growth in both of your abilities is undeniable. The resonance of your elemental clash echoed through the magical currents, a testament to the harmony you've achieved."

Kaelin and Lirael, still recovering, bowed respectfully. "Thank you, Master Elowen," they chorused.

Elowen gestured for them to rise and approached with a thoughtful expression. "Your control over your respective elements has reached new heights. Kaelin, your aquatic prowess, especially that tidal wave maneuver, was a force to be reckoned with. Lirael, the tri-elemental barrage showcased a seamless fusion of fire, earth, and wind. Truly commendable."

As the trio settled on the ground amidst the residual magic, Elowen, a beacon of knowledge, offered his insights. "Now, let's discuss your performance. Kaelin, your water-based attacks were creative and powerful.

However, in the next battle, focus on diversifying your offensive strategies. Surprise your opponents with unexpected combinations, and remember that adaptability is key."

Kaelin absorbed the advice with a nod, appreciating the guidance. Elowen then turned his attention to Lirael. "Your control over multiple elements is impressive, but ensure that your transitions between them remain fluid. Work on refining the synchronization of your elemental changes to maintain constant pressure on your opponents. And remember, precision in your illusions can be a potent weapon."

Lirael, showing determination, acknowledged the critique. Elowen continued, "Now, for the compliments. Kaelin, your defensive instincts, especially the water shield, saved you from a dire situation. Capitalize on this and further develop your defensive strategies. A well-balanced offense and defense make a formidable mage."

Kaelin nodded, absorbing the praise. Elowen then turned to Lirael. "Your aerial manoeuvrability was exceptional. The rising earth pillar showcased your adaptability in changing the battlefield to your advantage. Continue refining your spatial awareness and capitalize on the environment to gain the upper hand."

Lirael, fueled by the feedback, expressed gratitude. "Thank you, Master Elowen. We appreciate your guidance."

Elowen nodded. "Remember, the journey to mastery is a continuous one. Continue refining your strengths, addressing your weaknesses, and exploring new horizons in your magical abilities. The cosmic challenges ahead will demand nothing less."

As the trio continued their discussion, the training grounds remained a sacred space where the Triumvirate forged ahead on their shared path of growth and destiny.

In the aftermath of the intense magical exchange, the training grounds stood as a testament to the growing powers of the Triumvirate. Master Elowen, having observed their elemental clash, guided Kaelin and Lirael through reflections on their performance. As the echoes of their discussion lingered, a moment of contemplation settled over the trio.

Kaelin, curious about the deeper essence of his water-based abilities, turned to Master Elowen with a respectful inquiry. "Master Elowen, I've been pondering the significance of the water element. What does it truly represent in the world of magic and elemental affinity?"

Elowen, ever the sage, considered the question thoughtfully. "Water, in its essence, holds profound symbolism and qualities. Simplifying its representation, water signifies life, healing, and rejuvenation. It embodies the fluidity of movement and being in flow, much like the ever-changing currents of a river. Depth, emotions, and the subconscious are encapsulated within its essence."

Lirael, intrigued by the explanation, joined the conversation. "Master Elowen, does the water element also represent wisdom and self-reflection?"

Elowen nodded, acknowledging Lirael's insight. "Indeed, Lirael. Water, with its reflective nature, encourages introspection and self-discovery. It symbolizes transformation, rebirth, and adaptability. Like a river that navigates obstacles, those aligned with water find ways to overcome challenges with clarity and truth."

The sage's words resonated with Kaelin and Lirael, deepening their understanding of the elemental forces they wielded. Elowen continued, "In essence, your mastery over water extends beyond the manipulation of its physical form. It intertwines with the spiritual and emotional realms, offering a holistic prespective on its representation in magical affinity."

Encouraged by the newfound wisdom, Kaelin contemplated the symbolic weight of water in his magical journey. Lirael, too, embraced the multi-faceted nature of her elemental alignment. The training grounds, once a battlefield of elements, now became a sanctuary for the exploration of deeper magical insights.

As the trio lingered in the tranquil aftermath, a profound connection between the elements and their wielders unfolded—a connection that transcended the mere manipulation of magic. The elemental journey of Kaelin, Lirael, and the sage Elowen continued, each chapter unfolding a tapestry woven with the threads of growth, understanding, and the ever-present currents of magical destiny.

Encouraged by the newfound wisdom, Kaelin contemplated the symbolic weight of water in his magical journey. Lirael, too, embraced the multi-faceted nature of her elemental alignment. The training grounds, once a battlefield of elements, now became a sanctuary for the exploration of deeper magical insights.

As the trio lingered in the tranquil aftermath, a profound connection between the elements and their wielders unfolded—a connection that transcended the mere manipulation of magic. The elemental journey of Kaelin, Lirael, and the sage Elowen continued, each chapter unfolding a tapestry woven with the threads of growth, understanding, and the ever-present currents of magical destiny.

"If water represents life, adaptability, and transformation?" What does the other element represent Master?" asked Kaelin

Master Elowen, his gaze reflecting the depth of arcane wisdom, continued his elucidation on the essence of each element, expanding on their representations and significance.

"Beyond the individual traits, each element holds a broader tapestry of symbolism," he began, his voice carrying the weight of ancient knowledge. "Water, as you rightly recognized, embodies life, adaptability, and transformation. It is the source of rejuvenation, representing the ever-flowing cycle of existence. Water is also the mirror of our deepest emotions, the subconscious, and intuition. Its transformative nature reflects the constant evolution we experience in our journey."

Turning his attention to the flickering flame in the center, he continued, "Fire, in its essence, is the spark of passion that ignites our souls. It represents not only intensity and expressiveness but also the courage to face challenges fearlessly. Fire is the beacon of creativity and the driving force of life's endeavors. It symbolizes the transformative power within us, the ability to rise from the ashes and be reborn anew."

Master Elowen then shifted his focus to the solid ground beneath, "Earth, the stabilizing force, is the bedrock of existence. It represents not only stability and reliability but also the enduring resilience that allows us to weather life's storms. Earth is the repository of wisdom gained through patience and understanding of time. It symbolizes the nurturing embrace of the natural world, grounding us in the present while fostering growth."

As the breeze gently rustled the leaves, he continued, "Air, the intangible yet pervasive force, signifies versatility and freedom. It represents the adaptability to navigate the ever-changing currents of life. Air embodies the desire for independence and exploration, encouraging us to soar to new heights. It is the carrier of intellectual acuity, fostering analytical thinking and strategic planning."

Master Elowen paused, allowing the profound insights to settle. "Together, these elements create a harmonious balance, each complementing the other. The cosmic dance of water, fire, earth, and air weaves through the very fabric of existence, connecting all living things. Your mastery of these elements, individually and collectively, will unlock the secrets of the chronicle you are destined to weave."

As the echoes of his words lingered in the magical realm, the Triumvirate felt a deeper resonance with the elements they commanded. The training grounds, now infused with the essence of water, fire, earth, and air, became a sanctuary of wisdom, paving the way for the continued journey of Kaelin, Lirael, and Master Elowen in the cosmic tapestry of magic.

Master Elowen, sensing the eagerness within his disciples, decided to further illuminate the intricacies of elemental mastery through a demonstration of his own magical prowess. With a commanding yet serene presence, he gestured for Kaelin and Lirael to observe closely.

In a fluid motion, Master Elowen raised his hands, and the ambient magic responded to his command. The air around him shimmered, and the four elements—the very building blocks of the cosmos—answered his call. A gentle cascade of water droplets materialized, suspended in mid-air. Flames flickered into existence, dancing with controlled intensity. The earth beneath him seemed to resonate with a reassuring stability, and the air embraced him in a subtle breeze.

"Now, observe the harmony of the elements," Master Elowen spoke, his voice carrying a tranquil authority. "Water, ever-flowing and adaptable, dances with the flames of passion. Earth, the grounding force, provides a stable foundation for the swirling winds of change."

As the elements coalesced around him, Master Elowen demonstrated a seamless fusion of their powers. A shimmering sphere formed, encapsulating the four elements in perfect equilibrium. The water within sparkled with life, the flames emanated both warmth and intensity, the earth exuded unwavering stability, and the air whirled in a mesmerizing dance.

"In the chronicle of magic, the mastery lies not only in the command of individual elements but in the delicate dance between them," he explained. "Life's journey is a tapestry woven with the threads of water, the flames of passion, the solid foundation of earth, and the ever-changing winds of air. To harness their collective essence is to unlock the true potential of the arcane arts."

With a subtle gesture, the elemental sphere expanded, casting a kaleidoscope of colors across the training grounds. Each element retained its distinct identity yet contributed to the harmonious symphony of magic. The air was filled with a soothing melody, a testament to the unity inherent in the elemental forces.

As Master Elowen lowered his hands, the elemental display gradually dissipated, returning to the cosmic currents that permeated the magical realm. The training grounds, now bathed in a gentle luminescence, reflected the lingering resonance of the elemental demonstration.

"Remember, my dear apprentices," Master Elowen addressed Kaelin and Lirael, "your journey encompasses not only the mastery of individual elements but the art of weaving them together. The true magic lies in the balance you strike and the unity you forge within the cosmic dance of the elements."

With a profound nod, the Triumvirate acknowledged the depth of their mentor's teachings. The training grounds, having witnessed the convergence of elemental forces, stood as a testament to the boundless potential awaiting Kaelin, Lirael, and Master Elowen in the unfolding chronicle of magic.

# CHAPTER 25

# ELEMENTAL ALCHEMY – THE DANCE OF WATER AND AIR

As the Triumvirate delved deeper into the mysteries of magic, a new chapter unfolded in the realm of Eldermere—one that explored the intricate fusion of elemental forces. In their quest for mastery, Kaelin and Lirael sought to unlock the secrets hidden within the harmonious dance of water and air.

Under the guidance of Master Elowen, the duo ventured into the uncharted territories where the currents of water met the breezy whispers of air. The training grounds, infused with the residual energy of their previous elemental clash, became the canvas for a new experiment—Elemental Alchemy.

**Setting the Stage:**

Master Elowen, a sage of profound wisdom, stood at the center of the training grounds. His presence alone carried an air of anticipation as Kaelin and Lirael positioned themselves on opposite sides, ready to embark on a journey of elemental convergence.

The air was charged with magical potential, and the surroundings seemed to respond to the imminent fusion. The Triumvirate focused their energies, each attuned to the essence of their respective elements. Kaelin, the wielder of water's fluid might, and Lirael, the mistress of airy grace, prepared for the alchemical symphony that was about to unfold.

**The Dance Begins:**

Master Elowen, with a flicker of his secpter, initiated the dance. Water and air responded, intertwining in a delicate choreography that mirrored the ebb and flow of a cosmic waltz. Kaelin and Lirael mirrored the movements, their hands guided by an innate understanding of their elements.

The first manifestation was subtle—a mist that hung in the air, shimmering with the combined energies of water and air. As the dance intensified, the mist condensed, forming ethereal tendrils that wove through the atmosphere. The onlookers, attuned to the magical spectacle, could feel the temperature drop as the elemental alchemy took hold.

Master Elowen, having witnessed the successful fusion of water and air by Kaelin and Lirael, decided to delve further into the realms of Elemental Alchemy. With a gesture, he indicated the next phase of their training—a demonstration of a specific type of Elemental Alchemy, where water and air would intertwine in a different form.

Master Elowen's Prowess: As the Triumvirate gathered their focus, Master Elowen stepped forward, his scepter emanating a gentle glow. With a serene mastery over the elements, he began the dance of water and air. His movements were fluid, a seamless blend of precision and grace, as he invoked the energies that surrounded him.

## The Ethereal Mist:

In response to Master Elowen's command, a delicate mist began to weave through the air. Unlike the mist produced by Kaelin and Lirael's Elemental Alchemy, this mist bore a different essence—a hint of ethereality. It danced around Master Elowen, responding to his every thought.

The Triumvirate observed in awe as the mist gained substance, forming ephemeral shapes that echoed the mastery of both water and air. It seemed to shimmer with an otherworldly luminosity, embodying the enigmatic fusion orchestrated by their mentor.

## Manifestation of Elemental Essence:

With a final flourish, Master Elowen condensed the mist into small, radiant orbs. Each orb encapsulated the essence of both water and air, glimmering with the clarity of liquid and the weightlessness of wind. As he released the orbs into the air, they hovered in a mesmerizing display of elemental equilibrium.

"The Mist of Aether," Master Elowen announced, "represents the ethereal marriage of water and air. It carries the essence of both elements in perfect harmony, embodying the fluidity of change and the intangible freedom of the breeze."

## Triumvirate's Understanding:

Kaelin and Lirael absorbed the lesson with intent gazes, recognizing the depth of Elemental Alchemy. The Mist of Aether, with its radiant orbs, conveyed a profound truth about the potentiality of merging elements beyond their physical attributes.

Master Elowen encouraged them to interact with the Mist of Aether, guiding them to sense the unique qualities it possessed. Kaelin, with a touch, felt the cool embrace of water, while Lirael sensed the gentle currents of air. Together, they explored the ethereal dance that unfolded within the Mist of Aether, appreciating the intricate balance it held.

## A Lesson in Elemental Versatility:

Master Elowen, once again the sage imparting wisdom, addressed the Triumvirate. "Elemental Alchemy is a vast field of possibilities. The Mist of Aether is but one example of how water and air can converge in a form that transcends their traits. Remember, versatility in elemental fusion opens doors to solutions beyond the expected."

The training grounds, now adorned with the lingering essence of the Mist of Aether, became a reflection of the Triumvirate's expanding understanding of Elemental Alchemy. The Mist, with its radiant orbs, hovered like a testament to the infinite potentiality that awaited those who dared to explore the intricate dance of the elements.

With newfound knowledge, Kaelin and Lirael stood ready to continue their journey into the depths of Eldermere's magical tapestry, eager to unravel the mysteries that lay ahead in their shared destiny.

## Birth of Elemental Ice:

In a climactic crescendo, Kaelin and Lirael synchronized their movements, channeling the elemental dance to its peak. The mist, now charged with a frosty aura, solidified into a crystalline lattice. Ice, born from the fusion of water and air, adorned the training grounds in intricate patterns.

The elemental ice radiated a serene brilliance, capturing the essence of both water's adaptability and air's elusive freedom. Master Elowen observed with a twinkle in his eyes, acknowledging the newfound harmony within the Triumvirate's grasp.

## Mastering Elemental Ice:

As the elemental ice glistened under Eldermere's radiant sky, Master Elowen approached Kaelin and Lirael, commending their achievement. "You have unraveled the secrets of Elemental Alchemy. Ice, a testament to the synergy of water and air, embodies both the fluidity of change and the crystalline structure of stability."

He gestured for Kaelin and Lirael to interact with the ice, prompting them to explore its properties. Kaelin, with a touch, summoned a cascade of water from the ice, showcasing the fluid nature retained within its frozen form. Lirael, in turn, summoned a breeze that encased the ice in a fleeting dance, embodying the freedom of air.

## A Lesson in Elemental Fusion:

Master Elowen, now the orchestrator of this elemental convergence, imparted a crucial lesson. "Elemental Alchemy is not merely about merging powers; it's about discovering the unique qualities that arise from their union. Ice, in this instance, represents the delicate balance between change and stability. Embrace this lesson, for it will serve you well in the challenges that lie ahead."

The Triumvirate, now attuned to the dance of water and air, continued their exploration of Elemental Alchemy. The training grounds, adorned with elemental ice, became a symbol of the ever-evolving journey the Triumvirate undertook—a journey where magic, like a timeless dance, unfolded in harmonious synergy.

# CHAPTER 26

# MOONLIT ALCHEMY

That night under the full moon's glow, rest eluded Kaelin that night. The moon's whispers beckoned him to the shore, where the rhythmic dance of the sea's motion awaited beneath the silver radiance.

Immersed in the symphony of nature, Kaelin closed his eyes on the moonlit shores of Eldermere. The salty breeze carried the sea's essence, intertwining with memories that flooded his consciousness.

Guided by Master Elowen's wisdom, Kaelin felt a profound connection to the water element. Each tide against the shore was a reminder of the intricate dance of water molecules he sought to master. As the moon's glow bathed the scene, Kaelin's mind ignited with the realization that water, adaptable and transformative, held the key to manipulating matter.

Inspired, Kaelin wove the principles of elemental alchemy into his magical experimentation. Conjuring a spear from the night mist, he marveled at its liquid form. Before launching it towards a distant boulder, he delved into the untapped potential of elemental manipulation.

With meticulous control over temperature, Kaelin cooled the spear's tip, witnessing the crystallization into a frozen point of lethal precision. Simultaneously, he maintained the body of the spear in its liquid form, the water adapting to his command. Moonlight shimmered on the ever-changing surface.

Seeking innovation, Kaelin heightened the spear's base temperature. The liquid surged with newfound energy. To augment its trajectory, he enchanted the spear, a subtle yet powerful enhancement that propelled it with unimaginable speed.

As the moon bore witness, Kaelin, eyes still closed, unleashed the enchanted water spear. The projectile shot across the night, colliding with the boulder. The impact resonated through the calm waters, a symphony of power echoing through Eldermere. In the wake of his magical experimentation, Kaelin opened his eyes to behold the astonishing transformation he had wrought upon the distant boulder. What once stood as an unyielding monolith now bore a massive hole, a testament to the raw power and precision of his enchanted water spear.

The moonlight, now reflecting off the fractured surface of the boulder, illuminated the magical aftermath. The hole, a void carved into solid rock, spoke volumes of the elemental forces harnessed by Kaelin. It was not merely a puncture; it was a declaration—an assertion of mastery over the fundamental nature of matter.

Eldermere, ever the silent witness to the unfolding chronicle of magic, seemed to resonate with the energies unleashed. The sea, with its rhythmic ebb and flow, mirrored the ebb and flow of Kaelin's newfound abilities. The night, now imbued with the echoes of his magical prowess, held a profound stillness—a canvas upon which the mage inscribed his journey into the uncharted territories of elemental manipulation.

As Kaelin absorbed the visual manifestation of his achievement, a subtle smile played on his lips. The boulder, marked by the hole that now graced its core, stood as a monument to his evolving connection with the elements. It was a symbol of potential, a testament to the fusion of ancient knowledge and contemporary innovation.

In this nocturnal sanctuary, where the moon cast its gentle glow on the altered landscape, Kaelin embraced the silent applause of Eldermere. The night held secrets, and within those secrets, Kaelin found a path—one that led beyond the confines of tradition, toward the unexplored realms of magical discovery.

With the boulder's transformation etched into the silent narrative of Eldermere, Kaelin's magical journey continued under the watchful gaze of the moon and the embracing embrace of the sea—a mage, now marked by a hole in a boulder, but destined for boundless horizons in the realm of elemental mastery.

Amid his exhilaration, Kaelin's excitement was tempered by a realization—while his newfound power was undeniably fascinating, the extended casting time rendered it impractical for swift, real-time battles.

The dependency on a nearby body of water for optimal execution posed a significant tactical limitation.

Acknowledging the need for adaptability, Kaelin's mind began to churn with theories and possibilities. He recognized the imperative to evolve his magical arsenal into a more versatile form—one that would transcend the constraints of specific environmental conditions. With determination in his eyes, he meticulously listed out potential adaptations and enhancements to expedite his casting time and broaden the applicability of his water-based enchantments.

Among the considerations were

Considerations included:

## Condensed Elemental Form:

Exploring the concept of condensing the elemental forces within the water, Kaelin pondered whether he could streamline the process, allowing for quicker manifestation without compromising potency.

## Portable Aquifer Conduit:

Contemplating the creation of a portable aquifer conduit, Kaelin envisioned a magical container that could generate and store water temporarily, providing him with an on-the-go source for his aquatic spells.

## Catalytic Elemental Glyphs:

Experimenting with the integration of catalytic elemental glyphs, Kaelin mused on the potential of inscribing symbols that could expedite the transformation of water into various states, reducing the time required for complex manipulations.

## Symbiotic Enchantment Fusion:

Considering the amalgamation of symbiotic enchantments, Kaelin envisioned a harmonious fusion of his aquaforge blade's inherent powers with his elemental manipulations, creating a seamless integration that could enhance both offensive and defensive capabilities.

## Magical Resonance Amplification:

Exploring the amplification of magical resonance, Kaelin pondered whether he could attune his own magical signature to water, establishing a quicker and more responsive connection in the heat of battle. Renewed, Kaelin set forth on a journey of refinement, redefining his magical prowess. Under the moonlit night, he delved into elemental energies, a mage on the cusp of unlocking hidden mysteries.

Unbeknownst to Kaelin, Aqua, the water spirit, observed with astonishment. She whispered encouragement, promising her blessing if Kaelin could unlock a new spell, independent of a nearby water source.

As Kaelin immersed himself in the intricate dance of elemental energies under the moonlit night, unbeknownst to him, a gentle presence watched from the shadows. Aqua, the ethereal water spirit, observed with astonishment as Kaelin tirelessly endeavored to extract water essence from the very air around him.

Aqua marveled at the seer's determination, recognizing the depth of his connection to the water element. In the silvery glow of the moon, she whispered words of encouragement that carried on the night breeze, reaching Kaelin's ears like a subtle melody.

"Warrior-mage of the Waters, your pursuit is one of true dedication. May the moonlight guide your path, and the currents of magic unfold their secrets to you," Aqua murmured, her voice a gentle ripple in the magical atmosphere.

The water spirit, ever attuned to the ebb and flow of elemental forces, sensed the sincerity in Kaelin's endeavors. At that moment, she made a silent promise to herself. If the warrior could unlock the ability to create a new spell, one that didn't rely on a nearby water source, Aqua pledged to bestow upon him her divine blessing.

With a final gaze filled with ethereal grace, Aqua continued to observe Kaelin's efforts. The moonlight, acting as a celestial spotlight, illuminated the warrior's silhouette as he delved deeper into the mysteries of elemental magic. Unseen and unheard, the water spirit became a silent guardian, silently rooting for the warrior's success in unlocking the untapped potential hidden within the essence of the air itself.

# CHAPTER 27

# LIRAEL'S DETERMINATION

As the moon hung high in the night sky, casting its silvery glow upon Eldermere, Lirael stood on the outskirts of the magical training grounds. Her eyes were fixed on Kaelin, who was immersed in his experimental dance with the elements, pushing the boundaries of his magical prowess.

A teasing smile played on Lirael's lips as she watched Kaelin manipulate the water with precision and creativity. "Oh, Kaelin, you nerd," she teased, her words carrying a playful tone. Yet, beneath the jest, a spark of competitiveness ignited within her. She had always been driven by a desire to excel, to stand shoulder-to-shoulder with the best mages of Eldermere.

The air around Lirael crackled with a newfound determination. The witnessing of Kaelin's discoveries fuelled her inner fire. As a Triumvirate, they were bound by a shared destiny, and Lirael refused to lag. Her gaze intensified as she observed every subtle movement, every nuance in Kaelin's magical experimentations.

Amid her playful banter, Lirael's true feelings began to resurface. The camaraderie forged through shared challenges and victories had grown into something deeper. Beneath the teasing, a sense of admiration and connection blossomed within her heart. It was a realization that transcended mere rivalry.

As Kaelin continued to push the boundaries of elemental manipulation, Lirael felt a surge of determination coursing through her veins. The moon, witness to their magical endeavors, seemed to amplify the resolve within her. She took a step forward, ready to join the dance of elements, to unravel the mysteries that awaited her.

The mischievous spiritling scout—Emberkin, Geoling, Zephyrlet, observing from the shadows, sensed the shift in Lirael's aura. "Maybe it's her; maybe we have found our new candidate," Zephyrlet whispered to the other. With ethereal grace, they followed Lirael, intrigued by the burgeoning determination that radiated from the young mage.

## Lirael's Insight at Dawn:

As dawn painted the sky with hues of rose and gold, Lirael found herself standing at the precipice of newfound knowledge. The echoes of Kaelin's magical experimentation lingered in the air, and the tranquil morning carried with it a sense of revelation.

Approaching the magical training grounds, Lirael's demeanor was marked by a thoughtful expression. The playful banter of the night had given way to a more introspective contemplation. The competitive spark ignited by Kaelin's discoveries had kindled a different flame within her—a flame of insight and understanding.

Unlike Kaelin, whose meticulous experimentation continued into the night, Lirael approached the wealth of knowledge with a distinctive POV. She sought not only to master the elements but to weave them into a symphony uniquely her own. The predawn stillness provided a canvas for her thoughts to unfold.

With a gentle breeze carrying the whispers of the magical realm, Lirael closed her eyes, attuning herself to the ambient energies. The mischievous spiritlings observed her from a distance, curious about the direction her journey would take. As the first rays of sunlight bathed Eldermere in a warm embrace, Lirael began to move with purpose.

Her hands traced intricate patterns in the air, forming sigils that resonated with the essence of fire, earth, and wind. Each movement was deliberate, a dance that mirrored the ebb and flow of elemental forces. Unlike Kaelin's methodical approach, Lirael embraced fluidity and spontaneity, seeking inspiration from the world around her.

As the elements responded to her call, Lirael felt a profound connection to the magic that coursed through Eldermere. The fire manifested as a gentle warmth, the earth as a solid foundation beneath her feet, and the wind as a subtle caress that carried the promise of untold possibilities. The convergence of these elements painted a tapestry of harmony.

In this predawn dance, Lirael discovered that her magical prowess thrived on intuition and adaptability. She envisioned the elements not as separate entities but as interconnected strands in the vast tapestry of magic. The mischievous spirits, sensing the unique resonance of her approach, whispered words of encouragement in the air.

As the first light of dawn illuminated Eldermere's training grounds, Lirael opened her eyes, a reflection of newfound insight shining within them. The morning breeze carried the whispers of the mischievous spiritlings, acknowledging her unique journey into the heart of elemental magic.

In her quest to understand the individual nuances of her elemental affinity, Lirael sought inspiration from the intricate tapestry of nature. The morning sun painted the world with warm hues, and she found herself drawn to the heart of Eldermere's natural wonders.

Amidst the magical training grounds, Lirael observed the dance of the elements in the surrounding flora and fauna. The fire element revealed itself in the vibrant hues of blossoming flowers, each petal carrying a touch of the sun's radiant warmth. The earth manifested in the sturdy trunks of ancient trees, grounding themselves in the soil like pillars of stability.

The gentle breeze whispered secrets of the wind, rustling through leaves and carrying with it the essence of freedom. Lirael's eyes mirrored the reflection of a tranquil pond, where the water element mirrored the clear skies above, revealing the depth of its wisdom.

With a mindful gaze, Lirael began to weave her elemental dance. Her movements mirrored the swaying branches, and her gestures echoed the rhythm of the cascading waterfall nearby. As she immersed herself in the natural symphony, the mischievous spiritlings observed her with a newfound curiosity.

Lirael envisioned herself as an integral part of this harmonious composition, a conductor orchestrating the elements into a melody uniquely her own. The spiritlings, recognizing her sincerity, whispered encouragement in the wind, adding a magical cadence to her exploration.

In this dance with nature, Lirael sought not only to understand but to embody the essence of her elemental affinity. Each step, each gesture, was a dialogue with the world around her. The morning sun became her guide, and the elements responded to her silent inquiries.

As the magical training grounds transformed into a sanctuary of natural inspiration, Lirael's connection to her elemental affinity deepened. The dawn witnessed not just a mage in search of knowledge but a kindred spirit embracing the teachings of Eldermere's enchanting realm.

In the quiet moments of reflection, Lirael envisioned herself not only as a formidable force on the battlefield but also as a guardian, a nurturer of her allies' well-being. The gentle whispers of the wind seemed to echo the sentiment, guiding her towards a path of versatile mastery.

With this newfound perspective, Lirael embarked on a dual journey— to enhance her offensive capabilities while simultaneously exploring the realm of supportive magic. She sought to weave spells that would not only unleash the fury of her elemental powers but also provide solace and aid to Kaelin and their allies in the crucible of cosmic challenges.

Lirael's commitment to a dual-purpose mastery—attaining not only the heights of offensive might but also the subtleties of supportive enchantments. As the sun painted the sky with hues of promise, Lirael embraced her evolving role as both a fierce mage and a compassionate ally on the unfolding stage of their cosmic journey.

In the serene enclave of Eldermere, Lirael practiced harmonizing her magic with the essence of healing and protection. The mischievous spirits, curious observers of her evolution, witnessed the delicate balance she sought to achieve. As she conjured illusions of safety and mended the wounds of invisible adversaries, Lirael envisioned herself as a pillar of support in the magical tapestry of their shared destiny.

# CHAPTER 28

# HARMONY UNVEILED: ELEMENTAL REVELATIONS

As the sun bathed Eldermere in its golden embrace, Lirael found herself engaged in another sparring session with Kaelin. The air crackled with magical energy as Kaelin launched a swift attack, but to Lirael's surprise, her body moved with an almost instinctive grace. It was as if the natural elements themselves were guiding her every step.

In that fleeting moment of evasion, something extraordinary happened. Lirael felt a surge of magical power coursing through her veins, an unexpected boost to new heights. It was as if the elements acknowledged her connection and rewarded her with heightened abilities.

Seizing this newfound strength, Lirael unleashed a counterattack with unparalleled precision. Her magical prowess now seemed intertwined with the elements, and she harnessed the power of the sun, drawing energy from its radiant beams. The very ground beneath her seemed to vibrate with approval, responding to her every move.

As she weaved through the magical dance, Lirael became attuned to the subtle nuances of the natural elements surrounding her. The tiny vibrations in the ground became a source of insight, and the wind whispered secrets to her ears, guiding her in ways she had never thought possible.

Amid the battle, Lirael's mind became a canvas where the interconnectedness of the natural elements unfolded. She pondered how the earth, wind, sun, and even the gentle whispers of the air were connected. It was a revelation that went beyond the surface, delving into the very essence of elemental harmony.

With each dodge, each counterattack, Lirael explored the intricate tapestry of Eldermere's magic. The dance with Kaelin became not just a physical exchange but a communion with the elements. As she continued to battle, Lirael sought to understand how she could utilize the interconnectedness of nature to her advantage.

The sparring session became a transformative experience for Lirael, an awakening to the profound connection between the mage and the natural world. The sunlit battleground bore witness to her evolving understanding of elemental harmony, setting the stage for new possibilities in her magical journey.

In the aftermath of Lirael's remarkable display of elemental prowess, Kaelin, deep in thought, contemplated the intricacies of her movements. His analytical mind sparked a theory related to the essence of water present in the air around them. With a focused intent, he sought to experiment and validate his newfound understanding.

Drawing upon the moisture lingering in the atmosphere, Kaelin attempted to harness the water element. To his amazement, a small droplet began to coalesce at the tip of his blade. This tiny manifestation validated his theory – the very air held a reservoir of water essence, waiting to be tapped into.

Satisfied with this revelation, Kaelin decided to put his theory into action. He channeled his magical energy to highly pressurize the water droplet, transforming it into a projectile. With a swift and precise motion, he launched the compressed water straight towards Lirael.

As the water droplet dissipated into the air, Kaelin couldn't help but marvel at the untapped potential within the very atmosphere that surrounded them. This newfound understanding marked a pivotal moment in his magical journey, opening doors to innovative possibilities as he continued to explore the synergy between elemental forces and the unseen magic woven into Eldermere's air.

Reacting with instinctive agility, Lirael managed to dodge the high-speed water projectile just in the nick of time. The droplet whizzed past her, leaving a trail of shimmering mist in its wake. The skirmish between the two mages became an enchanting spectacle, an intricate ballet of elemental mastery.

Startled by Kaelin's innovative approach, Lirael's mind raced with newfound possibilities. The air around her whispered secrets of synergy, and she seized upon the realization that the elements could fuel one another. Concentrating intently, she harnessed the energy within the oxygen present in the air, infusing it into her fire-based magic.

With a determined focus, Lirael pointed her finger, and with a forceful exhale, she unleashed a scorching beam that cut through the air towards Kaelin. The beam, fueled by the energy drawn from the very atmosphere, manifested as a powerful extension of her elemental prowess.

In response to Lirael's fiery assault, Kaelin, quick on his feet, conjured a protective water barrier from the ambient moisture around him. However, in an unintentional twist, some parts of the barrier became supercooled and froze, forming an additional layer of ice. This impromptu ice layer proved to be a serendipitous defense, fortifying the water barrier against the intense heat of Lirael's attack.

The clash of fire and ice created a mesmerizing spectacle on Eldermere's magical training grounds. Lirael, surprised by the effectiveness of her adapted technique, marveled at the dynamic interplay between elemental forces. Kaelin, encased in his makeshift ice-enhanced barrier, recognized the untapped potential that lay within the delicate balance of elemental harmony.

As the remnants of their magical exchange dissipated into the air, both mages stood in contemplative awe. The realization that the very air they breathed held the key to augmenting their powers opened up a realm of possibilities, promising further revelations in their ongoing journey of elemental mastery.

Sitting side by side as the sun dipped below the horizon, Kaelin and Lirael indulged in a meal they had prepared together. The magical training grounds, now bathed in the soft glow of twilight, became the backdrop for an exchange of revelations and theories.

Kaelin, ever trusting of Lirael, wholeheartedly shared his theories on the interconnectedness of elements around them. Drawing inspiration from Master Elowen's Elemental Alchemy lessons, Kaelin wove together the strands of knowledge, connecting the dots between elemental forces. His eyes gleamed with enthusiasm as he articulated the intricate dance of water molecules, the fluidity of air currents, and the potential for synergies that transcended individual elements.

In response, Lirael reciprocated by unveiling her realizations. The harmony she discovered within the natural elements had sparked a profound understanding of how air, sunlight, and even the gentle whispers of the wind could amplify her magical prowess. The conversation flowed like a gentle stream, each revelation enhancing the other's POV on the boundless possibilities within their grasp.

As they shared their newfound insights, a sense of camaraderie deepened between them. The magical tapestry of Eldermere seemed to echo their excitement, casting a tranquil ambiance over their evening discussion. In the quietude of that moment, the duo forged not only a bond of friendship but also a shared commitment to unlocking the mysteries of elemental magic.

With the remnants of their meal lingering in the air, Kaelin and Lirael sat beneath the canvas of the evening sky, fueled by the collective knowledge and aspirations that intertwined in the enchanting realm of Eldermere.

As Lirael spoke about the connection of her power to the sun, Kaelin's eyes widened with realization. A spark of understanding illuminated his features, and he couldn't help but draw parallels to his own experiences. Reflecting on the night when he tested his spear attack on a boulder under the moonlight, a revelation unfolded within him.

"The moon," Kaelin mused, voicing his newfound insight. "I think my power is connected to the moon. The push and pull motion of the sea, always seeming too coincidental, and now that I think of it, my power first materialized and manifested under the moonlight."

In that moment of shared discoveries, a profound connection unfolded between Kaelin and Lirael. The moon and the sun, each holding sway over their respective powers, became celestial partners in the unfolding journey of these two mages within the enchanting realm of Eldermere.

Mind churning with theories, Kaelin listed adaptations and enhancements to expedite casting time and broaden water-based enchantments' applicability.

## Considerations included:

## Condensed Elemental Form:

Streamlining water's elemental forces for quicker manifestation.

## Portable Aquifer Conduit:

Creating a container generating temporary water for on-the-go spells.

## Catalytic Elemental Glyphs:

Inscribing symbols expediting water transformation.

## Symbiotic Enchantment Fusion:

Harmonizing aqua-forge blade powers with elemental manipulations.

## Magical Resonance Amplification:

Attuning magical signature to water for quicker connection.

## *New* Lunar Infusion Nexus:

Exploring the integration of lunar energies to enhance water-based enchantments, drawing inspiration from the moon's influence on tides.

## *New* Aqueous Nebula Synthesis:

Investigating the creation of a nebulous, water-based form for versatile magical applications, inspired by celestial phenomena.

### *New* Ripple Echo Forging:

Developing a technique to amplify water-based spells by creating ripple-like echoes, enhancing their impact.

### *New* Tidal Pulse Convergence:

Harnessing the rhythmic energy of tidal pulses to synchronize and empower water-based enchantments.

*New* Hydrokinetic Reservoir Integration:

Exploring ways to link personal magical reservoirs with water sources, ensuring a continuous and potent supply for spells.

After they had finished eating, Kaelin had a brilliant idea. "Maybe it's time for us to bring out our familiars," he suggested, his voice echoing with anticipation.

### Kaelin's POV:

Rising to his feet, determination blazing in his eyes, Kaelin summoned intricate magic circles. One pulsated with fiery hues for Ignix, the Aquanix Phoenix, and the other shimmered with ethereal radiance for Aqueon, the Aetherborne Guardian. The circles expanded, enveloping the familiars in a cascade of elemental energy, heralding a profound transformation.

### Ignix's POV:

From celestial heights, Ignix observed Kaelin's incantations. His fiery wings flickered with anticipation as he set forth a silent condition—a pact veiled in the radiance of his ethereal plumage. *"My existence itself is already a contradiction to this world,"* murmured Ignix, *his fiery wings shimmering with conflicting energies. "But Master Kaelin, who summoned me, gave me purpose."*

### Aqueon's POV:

Manifesting with an ethereal glow, Aqueon set forth a condition aligned with the advancement of Kaelin's abilities. *"I am an entity that exists only because of Master Kaelin's proficiency in enchantment and conjuration,"* Aqueon intoned with resonance. *"I will support him and his journey to master the art of enchantment and conjuration."*

As Eldermere's cosmic journey continued, Ignix and Aqueon stood as silent sentinels, their conditions echoing in the magical tapestry. The promise of transformative power lingered, awaiting the convergence of fire, water, and unspoken vows in a symphony of elemental evolution.

## Lirael's POV:

Lirael rose to her feet, the earth around her responding to the triple elements. Immersed in the dance of earth, sunlight, and wind whispers, she summoned Aero, attuned to elemental forces. The earth elemental took shape, its wings unfolding like delicate veils. In this moment of reunion, the bond between mage and familiar was deepened, marking a continuation of their mystical journey.

## Aero's POV:

*"In the sinuous rhythm of my master's enchantments, I find myself coiled in anticipation. Confined by the limitations of my dual nature, I'm a fragment of the grand tapestry. Yet, as that mysterious conjurer infuses his magic into me, a subtle tremor stirs. I become more than just a creature; I'm a living emblem, a manifestation of the intricate bond with my master's mastery—a testament to our shared journey. Like a bridge between realms, I connect Lirael's feelings to the ethereal presence."*

As whispers of approval echoed in the wind, a foreshadowing hinted at Aero's evolution into a majestic rainbow serpent, destined to hold dominion over all elemental powers.

## Kaelin's POV:

In the hushed embrace of Eldermere's enchanting realms, Kaelin turned toward Ignix, the Aquanix Phoenix, with an insatiable curiosity twinkling in his eyes. "Ignix," he mused, "can you unfurl the essence of your prowess? Show us the depths of your capabilities."

As Kaelin's request hung in the magical air, Ignix, the Aquanix Phoenix, began a celestial ballet of hydrokinetic mastery, manipulating water with mesmerizing precision. Liquid droplets danced around Ignix's radiant form, mirroring the intricate harmony between mage and familiar—a dance evolving within the enchanting realms.

This aquatic spectacle unfolded as a glimpse into the intricate dance between the Aquanix Phoenix and the elemental forces it now commanded. Each movement of Ignix's wings mirrored a harmony between mage and familiar, a dance that hinted at evolved capabilities and the ongoing journey within Eldermere's magical landscapes.

In response to Kaelin's encouragement, Ignix transitioned into a more assertive stance. With a commanding gesture, Kaelin prompted Ignix to unleash its Torrential Surge—a controlled deluge that cascaded with both grace and force. Liquid erupted from Ignix's wings, forming a powerful torrent that moved with precision, a vivid representation of the phoenix's advanced command over water.

Eagerly enthralled by Ignix's mesmerizing performance, Kaelin turned to Aqueon, his Aetherborne Guardian, with a spark of excitement in his eyes. Anticipation hung in the air as he encouraged Aqueon to showcase its unique abilities.

Aqueon responded with a shimmering glow, ready to unveil its own elemental prowess. With a humble yet powerful display, Aqueon conjured a Supportive Aegis—a magical field with a radius of 2 meters, forming beneath their feet. The ethereal energy radiating from the Aegis hinted at its potential to enhance enchantment and conjuring spells.

With fluid grace, Aqueon summoned numerous water droplets into the air, aligning them with precision. In a mesmerizing display, the droplets were then propelled directly at a distant boulder, showcasing both the guardian's control over water and its offensive capabilities.

Encouraged by the seamless execution, Aqueon, with humility, asked Kaelin to summon his recent experiment onto the field. In a surprising twist, Kaelin conjured the same spear concept he had experimented with the night before. To Kaelin's astonishment, the Aetherborne Guardian demonstrated the ability to summon up to 20 spears, each a manifestation of the concept Kaelin had crafted.

Witnessing the potent combination of Aqueon's supportive abilities and his conjuring prowess, Kaelin seized the opportunity. With focused intent, he directed the conjured spear familiars to soar through the air, launching a barrage of magical missiles at the distant boulder. The collaboration between mage and familiar unfolded as a testament to their growing synergy, marking a significant milestone in their shared journey through Eldermere's enchanting realms.

In the wake of this elemental display, a shared moment of profound connection unfolded between Kaelin and Ignix—a silent acknowledgment of the boundless possibilities that lay ahead in their magical journey within the enchanting realm of Eldermere.

"Remarkable!" Kaelin exclaimed, admiration evident in his voice. "Your combined prowess is beyond my expectations. Together, we are forging a formidable bond, and I can't wait to see how we'll continue to evolve and master the enchanting realms of Eldermere."

Ignix and Aqueon exchanged a glance, their eyes gleaming with a shared sense of dedication to their mage's journey. The trio, bound by magic and purpose, stood ready to face the mysteries that lay ahead in their enchanting adventure.

In the quiet recesses of his mind, Kaelin reached out to Ignix and Aqueon, urging them to communicate their abilities directly to his consciousness. He sought to forge a deeper understanding of their capabilities, envisioning a harmonious fusion that would give rise to a fighting style uniquely tailored to his essence. As the telepathic connection unfolded, the ethereal voices of Ignix and Aqueon resonated within Kaelin's thoughts, revealing the intricacies of their powers and paving the way for the emergence of a seamless and formidable combat strategy.

After witnessing the extraordinary capabilities of Ignix and Aqueon, Kaelin felt a profound sense of reassurance. The manifestation of their powers affirmed the validity of his theories and the intricate connection he shared with his familiars. However, a newfound challenge unveiled itself – the journey to unlock and harness the full potential of their abilities. While his theories proved accurate, the path to mastering and integrating these powers into a formidable force became the next thrilling chapter in his magical odyssey through Eldermere.

In the quiet recesses of his heart, Kaelin marveled at the confirmation of his theories. "So, it's true. I can use the essence of the air to conjure water particles as weapons," he acknowledged. Excitement surged through him as he envisioned the possibilities that lay ahead.

Taking out his notebook, Kaelin made necessary adjustments and added new details to further refine his water-based enchantments. The recent displays by Ignix and Aqueon had inspired him to expand his magical repertoire:

## Condensed Elemental Form:

Streamlining water's elemental forces for quicker manifestation.

## Portable Aquifer Conduit:

Creating a container generating temporary water for on-the-go spells.

## Catalytic Elemental Glyphs:

Inscribing symbols expediting water transformation.

## Symbiotic Enchantment Fusion:

Harmonizing aqua-forge blade powers with elemental manipulations.

## Magical Resonance Amplification:

Attuning magical signature to water for quicker connection.

## Lunar Infusion Nexus:

Exploring the integration of lunar energies to enhance water-based enchantments, drawing inspiration from the moon's influence on tides.

## Aqueous Nebula Synthesis:

Investigating the creation of a nebulous, water-based form for versatile magical applications, inspired by celestial phenomena.

## Ripple Echo Forging:

Developing a technique to amplify water-based spells by creating ripple-like echoes, enhancing their impact.

## Tidal Pulse Convergence:

Harnessing the rhythmic energy of tidal pulses to synchronize and empower water-based enchantments.

## Hydrokinetic Reservoir Integration:

Exploring ways to link personal magical reservoirs with water sources, ensuring a continuous and potent supply for spells.

## *New* Extended Supportive Field Extension:

Enhancing the Supportive Aegis to be utilized without summoning Aqueon into the physical realm. Through intense attunement, Kaelin can extend the magical field's influence even when Aqueon remains in the ethereal plane. This advancement allows for a seamless and immediate activation of the Supportive Aegis during battles without the need to bring Aqueon into the physical realm each time, ensuring continuous support in enchantments and conjuring spells.

## Harmony's Resurgence: Aerial Revelations

Lirael POV

After the morning sparring session and a shared meal, Lirael's request for Aero to showcase her abilities unfolded. Aero, in response, summoned her multifaceted Breeze Barrier, enveloping both Lirael and Kaelin in its protective and revitalizing embrace. The barrier's gentle breezes not only shielded them from potential harm but also carried with them a subtle yet potent healing effect.

As the soothing currents of Aero's magic surrounded them, the enchanting breeze worked its way through the fatigue that lingered in both Lirael and Kaelin. The revitalizing energy not only healed the wounds and strains accumulated during the intense sparring but also seemed to invigorate their very essence. Kaelin, who had joined them after the sparring session, felt a wave of rejuvenation coursing through him, dispelling the weariness that had settled after the morning's exertions.

The magical synergy between Aero's defensive and supportive abilities proved to be a well-timed boon, not only safeguarding them from harm but also restoring their vitality. The duo, fortified by the harmonious magic, stood ready for the adventures and challenges that awaited them in the enchanting realms of Eldermere.

In a mesmerizing display of elemental prowess, Aero, Lirael's devoted familiar, showcased its extraordinary abilities with seamless grace. The serpent continue with an enchanting demonstration of Aero-Earth Harmony, effortlessly weaving together air and earth elements in perfect unity. Its sinuous form is undulated with unparalleled grace, gliding through the air with ethereal fluidity and navigating the earthly terrain with otherworldly elegance.

Infused with Luminal enchantments, the serpent emanated a radiant aura, casting a soft and ambient glow that illuminated the surroundings. This Luminol Resonance not only enhanced its visual allure but also served a practical purpose, providing a constant source of gentle light that bathed the area in a soothing radiance.

Aerial Phasing, a remarkable ability, allowed the Aero to momentarily dissipate into the air, becoming partially intangible. This elusive maneuver rendered it difficult to target, showcasing its mastery over the elements and its innate ability to evade physical attacks.

In a display of both artistry and utility, Aero, unleashed Gust Serenade. Melodic gusts of wind enveloped the surroundings, creating a soothing serenade that had a calming effect on allies. Amidst the chaos of battle, this unique ability promoted focus and tranquility, further emphasizing the serpent's supportive role.

Adding alayer to its supportive abilities, the serpent revealed Zephyr's Grace—a healing grace bestowed upon allies. This gentle breeze of restorative energies mended wounds and revitalized those within its influence, showcasing the Zephyr Sentinel Serpent's dual nature as both guardian and healer.

In the quiet recesses of telepathic communication, Aero, the Zephyr Sentinel Serpent, chose to disclose her additional abilities directly to Lirael's mind. With a gentle mental whisper, Aero unveiled the secrets she had kept hidden, sharing the depths of her magical repertoire with her devoted mage.

Lirael, receiving these hidden revelations, marveled at the new found understanding of her familiar's abilities. The telepathic exchange strengthened the unspoken bond between mage and familiar, unveiling the mysteries that would further shape their journey through the enchanting realms of Eldermere.

As the display of magic by their familiars concluded, Kaelin and Lirael decided to send Ignix and Aero back to their respective realms. The aftermath of the magical showcase left a lingering sense of wonder in the air, the subtle glow of residual magic casting an ethereal ambiance around them.

"So, I remember you mentioned becoming Master Eldarion's pupil," Kaelin remarked, his eyes reflecting genuine curiosity.

Lirael, her mind buzzing with newfound possibilities, responded, "Oh yeah, why do you ask?" There was a spark in her eyes, a testament to her renewed passion for magical studies.

Kaelin considered Lirael's words, his thoughts running deeper than his spoken questions. "I was just wondering when you plan to start practicing with him. From what I heard, he's still recovering from using his Advanced Chronicle Weaving. It took a toll on him last time. Any plans?"

A thoughtful expression crossed Lirael's face. "Master Elowen mentioned that he has nothing else to teach me, but after discovering what my familiar can do and the revelations in our sparring sessions, there's so much more I want to learn. It has reignited my passion for magical studies. I'll organize my schedule to learn from both Master Elowen and Master Eldarion."

Kaelin nodded, acknowledging the importance of continuous learning. "Our mastery of the elements may be above average, but there's still much we don't understand about magic. And then there's Aether. Master Elowen did mention something about Luminara or should I say Eldermere. Now that we know the history, how can we harness it? After the trial and our successful conjuring of familiars, I feel like I've found a way to access it again. Master Elowen needs to teach us."

In the distance, Master Elowen let out a sudden sneeze, drawing their attention. "Achoooo...! I think I forgot something very important. Well, if it's not worth remembering, maybe it's worth nothing," he said, wiping his nose, his absent-minded demeanor intriguing.

Lirael suggested, "Let's go and see him after this. Right now, I'm going back to take a rest." Her words carried a sense of determination, a readiness to delve into the mysteries that awaited them.

"Okay, then. See you again, Lirael," Kaelin bid farewell, watching as Lirael walked away, each step echoing her renewed commitment to magical exploration.

# CHAPTER 29

# THREADS OF LAUGHTER, SHADOWS OF DESTINY

As Kaelin and Lirael walked through the magical enclave, the soft glow of the orbs casting a gentle radiance, Kaelin couldn't help but grin. "Well, that was quite the day, wasn't it? Who knew my attempt at magical water projectiles would turn into such a spectacle?" Lirael chuckled, shaking her head.

"You certainly know how to make an impression, Kaelin. I never thought I'd be dodging water amid magical training. But hey, it was a good test of my reflexes." Kaelin playfully nudged her shoulder. "And your dodge was as impressive as your magical prowess, my fellow apprentice. We make quite the magical duo, don't we?"

Lirael raised an eyebrow. "Magical duo? I think you mean magical troublemakers." They both laughed, the camaraderie between them evident in their banter. The magical enclave resonated with the echoes of their shared laughter, a brief interlude of lightness amid arcane mysteries.

As they approached Master Elowen's dwelling, the tone shifted. The anticipation of what lay ahead tempered their playful banter, casting a subtle shadow over their steps.

The soft radiance of the orbs now seemed to dance with a more mysterious energy. Upon entering, Lirael, her eyes gleaming with excitement, addressed Master Elowen, "Master Elowen, may we have your attention regarding a discovery we made today?" Master Elowen, intrigued, raised an eyebrow, signaling the transition from banter to the serious matter at hand. "Of course, Lirael. What have you unearthed?"

Lirael began recounting the morning's events, her unintentional fusion of solar energy and wind magic. Simultaneously, Kaelin seized the opportunity to share his moonlit experimentation and the theory about the ambient essence of water in the air.

The expressions on Master Elowen and Eldarion's faces shifted from curiosity to astonishment. They exchanged a swift glance, recognizing an unexpected advancement in their apprentices' magical prowess.

Master Elowen, composing himself, turned to Kaelin. "So, you aimed a condensed water projectile at Lirael?" he inquired, a mix of surprise and concern in his voice. Kaelin, caught slightly off guard, nodded hesitantly. "Yes, sir." Before Master Elowen could respond, a quick dodge from Kaelin and a playful smack from Eldarion ensued, resuming a moment of banter amidst the serious discussion.

Amidst the banter, Lirael, with a gentle smile, came to Kaelin's defense. "Master, Sir Eldarion, it was an inventive test. Kaelin's innovative approach inspired me to explore the harmonious combination of elemental forces. The power of the sun, wind, and earth guided me safely through his experimentation." The realization dawned on Master Elowen and Eldarion, and they exchanged amused glances.

Eldarion couldn't help but tease Kaelin with a remark about his denseness resembling someone they both knew.

"Kaelin," Master Elowen said, his tone shifting from seriousness to a hint of amusement, "while your discovery is remarkable, remember the importance of discretion in magical experimentation. What if Lirael hadn't dodged? Always be mindful of potential consequences, especially in uncontrolled environments."

As the realization set in, Kaelin turned red with embarrassment. Lirael, sensing his discomfort, tried to lighten the mood, and Eldarion, unable to resist, added a teasing remark. "Kaelin, you're as clueless as your father once was, testing magic without considering the aftermath," Eldarion chuckled, earning a playful glare from Kaelin.

The scene concluded with an air of camaraderie, lessons learned, and the promise of more magical revelations to come. The banter seamlessly interwoven with the gravity of their magical discoveries and the impending challenges that lay ahead. The laughter in the room slowly subsided, giving way to a focused exchange of knowledge.

Master Elowen, still with a twinkle in his eye, steered the conversation back to the discoveries at hand. "Your revelations about harnessing energy from celestial bodies and manipulating the ambient elemental essence are intriguing, indeed," he remarked. "These are advanced techniques, and it seems you both have inadvertently tapped into profound aspects of magic." Eldarion, now composed, added his insights. "The synergy between the elements and celestial bodies is a delicate dance. Mastering it requires finesse and understanding. It seems Eldermere itself guides you on this journey of discovery."

Encouraged by their mentors' approval, Kaelin and Lirael felt a renewed sense of purpose. "We're eager to learn more," Kaelin said, his earlier embarrassment transforming into determination. Lirael added, "Our familiars have also shown remarkable abilities that align with these discoveries. Aero, my Zephyr Sentinel Serpent, has showcased an intricate harmony of air and earth elements.

It's as if Eldermere itself responds to our exploration." Master Elowen nodded thoughtfully. "Your familiars are manifestations of your magical essence. Their abilities reflect the depth of your connection to Eldermere's magical weave. This journey you're on is not just about mastering spells; it's about understanding the very essence of the realm we inhabit." As the apprentices and their mentors continued their discussion, the room became a sanctuary of shared wisdom.

Master Elowen and Eldarion, recognizing the potential within Kaelin and Lirael, outlined the next steps in their magical education. The Chronicles of Eldermere awaited their skilled weavings, and the enchanting journey into the heart of magical mysteries continued. The night unfolded with a blend of earnest learning, unexpected discoveries, and moments of levity. The room, now wrapped in the mystical ambiance of magical discourse, resonated with the echoes of whispered secrets and untold possibilities.

The Chronicles, ancient and waiting, beckoned the apprentices to delve deeper into the enchanting tapestry that was Eldermere's magical legacy. The atmosphere shifted once more, the weight of ancient prophecies and imminent challenges casting a shadow over the room. The laughter and banter, though momentarily set aside, had served as a brief respite before the apprentices embarked on the path that would define their roles in the unfolding destiny of Eldermere.

As the weight of Eldermere's destiny settled upon the room, Master Elowen, with a solemn expression, turned his attention to the apprentices. The magical glow of the orbs intensified, casting intricate shadows across the ancient tomes and artifacts that adorned the room.

"The Chronicles you carry, Lirael, and the innate connection Kaelin shares with Eldermere's essence suggest a bond beyond mere apprenticeship," Master Elowen spoke, his words echoing with ancient wisdom. "The time has come to unravel the deeper mysteries of your abilities and the purpose that binds you to Eldermere's fate."

Eldarion, standing like a sentinel of Aether, added, "The shadows we face are not to be underestimated. They are remnants of forgotten realms, echoes of ancient conflicts. Your familiars, Ignix and Aero, hold the key to understanding and, perhaps, mending the fabric of Aether itself."

Kaelin and Lirael exchanged determined glances, a silent affirmation of their shared commitment. The revelation of a greater purpose had ignited a spark within them, transcending the boundaries of individual growth.

"As you delve into the Chronicles, remember that the threads of destiny are interwoven with your actions. Each spell, each discovery, is a stitch in the tapestry of Eldermere's existence," Eldarion emphasized, his gaze penetrating the apprentices' very beings.

Master Elowen, with a sweep of his hand, summoned a shimmering projection of Eldermere—a celestial realm bathed in radiant energies. The intricate dance of magical threads illuminated the vast expanse, revealing the ebb and flow of Aether's currents.

"The Chronicles are not merely conduits for spells; they are gateways to Eldermere's essence. Through them, you can discern the ephemerality of time, perceive the echoes of bygone eras, and tap into the very lifeblood of Aether," Master Elowen explained, his eyes reflecting the vast depths of magical knowledge.

Kaelin and Lirael approached the projection, their fingers lightly tracing the threads that crisscrossed the magical realm. The Chronicles responded to their touch, resonating with an energy that seemed attuned to the heartbeat of Eldermere itself.

"Now, the journey unfolds," Eldarion declared, his voice resonating with a harmonious blend of caution and encouragement. "Through your familiars, through the Chronicles, you shall pierce the veil of shadows and unveil the truths that lie at the heart of Eldermere."

Master Elowen concluded, "This is not merely a quest for mastery; it is a quest to restore equilibrium, to safeguard Eldermere from the encroaching shadows. Embrace the mysteries, young mages, for your destinies are intricately woven with the fate of this enchanted realm."

As the echoes of their mentors' words faded, Kaelin and Lirael stood before the magical projection, ready to embark on a journey that transcended the realms of magic and destiny. The Chronicles of Eldermere awaited their skilled weavings, and the enchanting tale of unraveling shadows had just begun.

The night continued its silent watch as the apprentices, guided by the wisdom of Masters, prepared to confront the challenges that awaited them in the heart of Eldermere's mysteries.

# CHAPTER 30

# NEXUS OF HARMONIES

In the hallowed chamber of magical discourse, Master Elowen, his eyes carrying the weight of ancient wisdom, observed Kaelin with a discerning gaze. Sensing the latent power within Kaelin's magical essence, Master Elowen prompted, "Kaelin, summon forth your familiar, Ignix, and let Aqueon grace this sacred space."

Kaelin, recognizing the significance of the request, focused his energy. With a wave of his hand and an incantation that echoed through the chamber, Ignix, materialized, its fiery and aqueous form blending seamlessly. At Kaelin's side, Aqueon, a testament to the harmonious fusion of enchantment and conjuration, radiated a quiet strength.

As the ethereal entities took their place, Master Elowen continued the unveiling. With a commanding presence, he summoned his own familiar—the Aetherial Phoenix. The majestic creature emerged in a blaze of ethereal flames, casting a radiant glow across the room. Beside it, a collective manifestation known as the Ethereal Guardians stood, their forms flickering like ephemeral stars.

Master Elowen, with a subtle yet profound flourish, introduced a new creation born from collaboration—the Aetherial Nexus Warden. "Through the synergy of the Aetherial Phoenix and the Ethereal Guardians, the Aetherial Nexus Warden emerges—an enchanting guardian embodying the essence of Aetherial Nexus Mastery.

It stands as a testament to the harmonious collaboration between Lumarian and ethereal entities." The room resonated with the magical presence of the familiars and conjured entities, each embodying the unique mastery and collaboration of their respective mages. The apprentices, Kaelin and Lirael, witnessed not only a display of magical prowess but a glimpse into the profound possibilities that awaited them on their journey into the heart of Eldermere's mysteries. Master Elowen, with a thoughtful nod, turned to his familiar, the Aetherial Phoenix, and spoke in a resonant tone, "Aetherial Phoenix, weave the threads of Aether and conjure a protective barrier around us.

Let the essence of Lumarian and ethereal magic intertwine to form a shield against the unseen." The majestic Aetherial Phoenix unfurled its wings, and with a regal sweep, it began to channel the energies of Aether.

Ethereal flames danced around the room, coalescing into a shimmering barrier that encircled the apprentices and their mentors. Simultaneously, Master Elowen addressed the Ethereal Guardians, "Summon forth your vigilant underling to stand guard.

Let their ethereal presence watch over us and alert us to any disturbances in the magical currents." The Ethereal Guardians, in a harmonious display of unity, extended their otherworldly forms, and from their midst emerged a smaller ethereal entity—a guardian attuned to the magical vibrations of Eldermere.

Positioned strategically, the ethereal underling stood as a silent sentinel, ready to respond to any shifts in the mystical currents that surrounded them. With the protective barrier in place and the ethereal underling standing guard, the chamber became a haven guarded by Lumarian and ethereal entities. Master Elowen, satisfied with the additional safeguards, turned his attention back to Kaelin and Lirael, his gaze reflecting a blend of mentorship and anticipation for what lay ahead in the unraveling tapestry of Eldermere's mysteries.

Lirael, catching the current of magical momentum, focused her energy on summoning her familiar, Aero—the Zephyr Sentinel Serpent. With a graceful gesture and an incantation that echoed through the enchanted chamber, Aero materialized, its serpentine form undulating with an ethereal grace.

The air around them seemed to shimmer as Aero's presence brought a subtle harmony of air and earth elements into the room.

Eldarion, not to be outdone, joined the summoning ritual. His mastery over Aether resonated as he summoned the Ethereal Scholar, a manifestation embodying the essence of all four elements. The Ethereal Scholar, with its ever-shifting form representing air, water, earth, and fire, added a profound layer of elemental wisdom to the gathering.

As Aero and the Ethereal Scholar took their places beside their summoners, the room became a tableau of magical entities—a convergence of familiars, conjured beings, and ethereal guardians. The air hummed with the energies they collectively brought, and the magical enclave seemed to pulse with an otherworldly vibrancy.

Lirael and Eldarion exchanged a knowing glance, a silent acknowledgment of the power they had conjured. With their familiars and ethereal entities standing by their sides, the apprentices and mentors were now united, ready to face the mysteries that awaited them in the heart of Eldermere.

The Chronicles of Eldermere lay open before them, and the next chapter of their journey was poised to unfold. Eldarion, in tune with his instincts, whispered a command to his familiar, the Ethereal Scholar.

With a shimmering aura, the Scholar extended its influence, weaving the fabric of magic to create an invisible field around the room. This protective enchantment was designed to deter unwanted intrusions and serve as an ethereal barrier against external influences.

The air itself seemed to respond to the Scholar's conjuration, creating an imperceptible yet potent shield around the gathering. Eldarion, reassured by the Scholar's ethereal vigilance, felt a sense of security settle over the room. "Thank you, my friend," Eldarion acknowledged the Scholar, its elemental essence resonating with the Aether Master's gratitude. With the protective field in place, the apprentices and mentors could delve into their discussions without fear of interruption.

The Chronicles of Eldermere awaited their exploration, and the room, now guarded by ethereal forces, became a sanctum of shared wisdom and magical discourse. The journey into the heart of Eldermere's mysteries continued, shielded by the collaborative efforts of familiars, ethereal entities, and the skilled mages who summoned them.

Master Elowen, satisfied with the preparations, turned his attention back to Kaelin and Lirael. The room, now secure in its mystical seclusion, provided the perfect setting for the unraveling of magical secrets. "Let us resume our exploration."

The apprentices, flanked by their familiars and ethereal companions, delved into the enchanted pages, ready to unlock the secrets that would shape their destinies and the fate of Eldermere. The night continued its silent vigil, witnessing the convergence of magical forces and the forging of bonds that transcended the realms of reality.

In the enchanted chamber, surrounded by the radiant glow of summoned entities and ethereal guardians, Master Elowen guided Kaelin and Lirael toward the Chronicles of Eldermere. The ancient tomes seemed to pulse with the accumulated wisdom of centuries, their mystical pages beckoning the apprentices to unravel the secrets within.

As the apprentices delved into the Chronicles, their familiars and ethereal companions stood guard, their presence contributing to the harmonious atmosphere that enveloped the room. The air hummed with the magical currents, resonating with the intertwined energies of Lumarian and ethereal magic.

Master Elowen, with a keen eye, observed the apprentices' interactions with the Chronicles. "Remember," he cautioned, "the Chronicles are more than mere texts. They are conduits to the very essence of Eldermere. Through them, you can perceive the threads of destiny, tap into ancient knowledge, and unveil the truths that lie at the heart of our enchanted realm."

Kaelin and Lirael, guided by the master's words, allowed the Chronicles to weave their magic around them. The pages revealed intricate diagrams of celestial patterns, ancient incantations that resonated with the elements, and prophecies that hinted at the apprentices' roles in the unfolding destiny of Eldermere.

As the apprentices immersed themselves in the Chronicles, a subtle resonance echoed through the chamber. The Aetherial Nexus Warden, Master Elowen's conjured entity, seemed to be attuned to the ancient tomes. Its ethereal presence added a layer of mystical significance to the apprentices' exploration.

Eldarion, sensing the ethereal currents, approached the Chronicles alongside his familiar, the Ethereal Scholar. The Scholar, embodying the essence of air, water, earth, and fire, lent its elemental insights to the pages. Eldarion's eyes gleamed with anticipation as he deciphered the arcane symbols and writings that adorned the Chronicles.

Lirael, guided by the harmonious essence of her Zephyr Sentinel Serpent, Aero, discovered a section that resonated with her affinity for air and earth magic. Aero's serpentine form undulated with excitement as Lirael traced the ancient glyphs, unlocking a deeper understanding of the wind and earth elements.

Kaelin, attuned to the fusion of fire and water within his Ignix-Aquanix Phoenix and Aqueon, found a passage that hinted at the synergy between opposing elements. The Chronicles illuminated the potential for unprecedented magical fusion, and Kaelin's eyes sparkled with new found inspiration.

Master Elowen, observing the apprentices' discoveries, nodded approvingly. "The Chronicles respond to your magical essence. They recognize the threads of destiny woven within you. Continue to explore, for the knowledge within these tomes is a gift from Eldermere itself."

As the apprentices continued their exploration, the protective barrier held firm, and the ethereal underling stood vigilant, attuned to the magical currents. The Aetherial Nexus Warden, a silent guardian, exuded an aura of Lumarian and ethereal mastery, adding a touch of enchantment to the atmosphere.

Eldarion, still in tune with his instincts, whispered to the Ethereal Scholar. The Scholar extended its influence further, creating an ethereal projection that hovered over the Chronicles, highlighting passages of particular significance. Eldarion's gaze followed the Scholar's guidance, revealing hidden depths within the ancient tomes.

Lirael, captivated by the wind and earth revelations, began to experiment with subtle wind magic, guided by Aero's ethereal presence. The air in the chamber responded to her commands, creating gentle breezes that resonated with the elemental harmony she sought to master.

Kaelin, inspired by the potential fusion of fire and water, initiated a magical dance with his Ignix-Aquanix Phoenix and Aqueon. Flames and aqueous currents intertwined in a mesmerizing display, echoing the profound connection between the opposing elements.

Master Elowen, recognizing the apprentices' attunement to the Chronicles, allowed a faint smile to play on his lips. The unfolding scene, a dance of magic and discovery, affirmed the apprentices' roles in Eldermere's intricate tapestry.

The Chronicles of Eldermere, ancient and alive, revealed glimpses of forgotten realms, prophecies, and the interconnected destinies of those who dared to delve into their mysteries. The enchanted chamber resonated with the convergence of Lumarian and ethereal magic, as the apprentices continued their journey into the heart of Eldermere's secrets.

The night, a silent witness to the magical discourse, embraced the apprentices and their mentors in a cocoon of mystical energy. The next chapter of their journey awaited, and the pages of the Chronicles turned with the promise of revelations that would shape the fate of Eldermere.

Lirael, guided by the harmonious essence of her Zephyr Sentinel Serpent, Aero, discovered a section that resonated with her tri-elemental affinity— air, earth, and fire. Aero's serpentine form undulated with excitement as Lirael traced the ancient glyphs, unlocking a deeper understanding of the interconnected forces of the wind, earth, and fire elements.

Kaelin, attuned to the soothing flow of water within his Ignix-Aquanix Phoenix and Aqueon, found a passage that hinted at the synergy between opposing elements. The Chronicles illuminated the potential for unprecedented magical fusion, emphasizing the delicate dance between water and opposing forces. Kaelin's eyes sparkled with newfound inspiration as he considered the intricate balance within the realm of water magic.

Kaelin, immersed in the rhythmic currents of water magic, delved deeper into the Chronicles. A section caught his attention, revealing the mastery of water in its various states—liquid, solid, and vapor. The ancient text spoke of the fluid nature of water magic, describing how skilled mages could manipulate water in its different forms, harnessing its adaptability and transformative properties.

As Kaelin read on, he encountered passages that drew a connection between water magic and the moon's influence. The Chronicles unveiled the profound interplay between the phases of the moon and the ebb and flow of water magic. Lunar cycles, it seemed, held a key to unlocking the true potential of water manipulation.

The revelation sparked a surge of curiosity within Kaelin. Contemplating the moon's impact on water elements, he envisioned a dance of energies that transcended the ordinary boundaries of magic. The delicate balance within the realm of water magic extended beyond mere manipulation; it embraced a symbiotic relationship with celestial forces, particularly the moon, opening up avenues for unparalleled mastery.

Amidst the delicate dance with the Chronicles, Eldarion's practiced eyes discerned a scroll tucked away in a corner, its edges tinged with the passage of time. As an experienced archaeologist, he recognized the significance of seemingly overlooked details. Retrieving the scroll with a mixture of curiosity and excitement, Eldarion delicately unfurled its ancient pages. To the astonishment of those gathered, the scroll detailed the very artifact mentioned in the *prophecy*—the key to unlocking the mysteries of Eldermere. Eldarion, with a gleam in his eyes, shared the contents with the apprentices and mentors.

It hints at a legacy, a connection that goes beyond the confines of time. Lirael, your familiar's presence is woven into the very fabric of Eldermere's history." Lirael, her eyes widening with fascination, approached the scroll. The intricate depictions echoed the sinuous form of Aero, the Zephyr Sentinel Serpent. The realization that her familiar held a place in the ancient tapestry of Eldermere's mysteries filled Lirael with a profound sense of purpose.

Master Elowen, his gaze transitioning between the scrolls and the apprentices, recognized the significance of these newfound revelations. The chamber, now filled with the echoes of prophecies and the wisdom of ages, became a sanctuary of shared knowledge and anticipation. As the night unfolded, the apprentices and mentors continued to explore the Chronicles, guided by the insights gleaned from the discovered scrolls. The enchanted chamber, once silent, now buzzed with the energy of revelation and the promise of a destiny intertwined with the essence of Eldermere itself.

Amid their exploration, Eldarion, with his experience as an archeologist, discovered another scroll tucked away in a hidden compartment. Intrigued, he carefully unfurled the parchment, revealing ancient inscriptions detailing the evolution of familiars and their profound connection to their masters' wishes and emotions.

"Look here," Eldarion beckoned to the gathered assembly, "this scroll reveals the evolution of familiars—a manifestation of their connection to the heartfelt wishes and aspirations of their masters. It is a testament to the bond we share with our enchanted companions, a bond that transcends the mere casting of spells." Kaelin and Lirael, with newfound understanding, exchanged glances that mirrored the deep connection they held with their familiars. Aero and Ignix, ethereal entities embodying their masters' aspirations, seemed to resonate with the ancient wisdom contained within the scrolls. In a further revelation, Eldarion uncovered a serpent-themed scroll, its illustrations bearing a striking resemblance to Lirael's Zephyr Sentinel Serpent, Aero. Eldarion's voice resonated with awe as he addressed the assembly. "Look closely, my friends. This serpent scroll shares uncanny similarities with our dear Aero.

As Eldarion read aloud, he stumbled upon a section that spoke of serpents as unique beings tied intimately to their masters. The serpent's existence, it explained, primarily embodied the prowess of its master and, secondarily, formed a connection with the emotions of others, influenced by the master's feelings. The full potential of the serpent's abilities could be unlocked through the master's desires and emotional states.

While reading this revelation, Eldarion's cheeks flushed, and a subtle warmth spread across his face. Realizing the implications of the passage, he continued reading aloud with a shy demeanor. Unbeknownst to him, Lirael, absorbed in her exploration and attuned to the emotions around her, detected the subtle change in Eldarion. As she comprehended that the passage was describing Aero, her Zephyr Sentinel Serpent, a blush crept across her cheeks.

Meanwhile, Kaelin, engrossed in the Chronicles and oblivious to the unfolding dynamics, marveled at the fascinating information he was uncovering. The soft glow of magical orbs surrounded him as he remained immersed in his world of discovery, completely unaware of the shared glances and unspoken exchanges happening in the enchanted chamber.

The chamber, filled with the soft glow of magical orbs and the hum of ethereal energies, became a sanctuary of shared knowledge. Lirael, now blushing at the realization, exchanged a knowing glance with Aero. The magical enclave had become a space where the past and present intertwined, unraveling the secrets that connected the apprentices to the profound legacy of Eldermere.

# CHAPTER 31

# SECRETS IN THE ENCHANTED CHAMBER

**Eldarion's POV:**

Twenty year ago amidst the ancient tomes and the glow of magical orbs, Umbralis, the Umbral Alchemist, stood with a face full of regret. As Eldarion, the Luminara Archaeologist, summoned his Ethereal Scholar named Atticus and erected a magical barrier sensitive to disturbances, Umbralis felt a sense of relief wash over him. For the first time in what seemed like an eternity, he felt the comforting embrace of a haven.

With a sigh, Umbralis finally let his guard down. The weight of his possession and the burden he carried seemed to lift, if only for a moment. The ethereal atmosphere in Eldarion's tent, protected by Atticus' magical barrier, offered a sanctuary where Umbralis could begin to unravel the tangled threads of his recent struggles.

As Umbralis allowed himself to relax, a wave of exhaustion swept over him. The relentless battle for control had taken its toll on his spirit. He felt a subtle warmth from the magical energies within the protective barrier, a reassurance that he was now in safe hands.

In a moment of vulnerability, Umbralis, overcome by fatigue, finally fainted. Eldarion, ever watchful, gently guided Umbralis to one of the beds in the tent. Atticus, the Ethereal Scholar, hovered nearby, ready to assist in any way necessary.

Five days passed, and finally, Umbralis began to stir. His eyes opened slowly, and he found himself surrounded by the gentle glow of magical orbs. Erebus, his loyal familiar, remained vigilant at his side, a shadowy guardian in the ethereal realm.

Umbralis looked around, his gaze meeting Eldarion's. A mixture of gratitude and realization flickered in his eyes. "Eldarion," he began, his voice carrying the weight of recent revelations, "I cannot thank you enough for providing me with a haven in this tumultuous time."

With a composed demeanor, Umbralis began to explain the events that had transpired. He revealed an ancient artifact he had discovered, an artifact that had become the catalyst for his possession by an evil entity. Umbralis shared the fragmented memories—of a plan conceived in his locked state, of glimpses into Master Voss's true identity, and of the looming threat that still hung over Eldermere.

"I realized that the only way to come clean and set things right was to trust someone," Umbralis confessed. "That someone was you, Eldarion. You, with your unique connection to the elements and your understanding of chronicles, became the anchor I desperately needed."

In the present, Eldarion's eyes conveyed determination. *"I've done my part, and now everything is up to your plan, Umbralis"* he whispered, alluding to a higher purpose that he was yet to fully comprehend. The chamber, steeped in magical energies, bore witness to a pivotal moment in Eldermere's unfolding saga.

As Umbralis continued to narrate the events that led to his possession and his plan to thwart Master Voss, Eldarion listened attentively. The revelation brought a new layer of complexity to their journey, intertwining fate, ancient artifacts, and the interconnected destinies of those who dared to delve into the mysteries of Eldermere.

With Umbralis back to his true self, a sense of relief washed over the enchanted chamber. Eldarion, always attuned to the nuances of fate, could feel the weight of recent events in the air. As Umbralis, fully aware of Master Elowen's nature and the potential consequences of his plan, leaned in closer, the gravity of the situation became palpable.

"Eldarion," Umbralis began, his tone serious yet filled with gratitude, "I must entrust you with a secret—one that Elowen must not know. I fear he would try to stop me, and the fate of Eldermere hangs in the balance."

Umbralis, with sincerity in his eyes, continued, "Continue your pursuits as an archaeologist, indulge in your hobbies, but eighteen years from now, return to Luminara. Together with Master Elowen, guide the chosen warriors—a boy blessed by water and pure Aether, a girl with a tri-elemental affinity of fire, earth, and air, and a unique chronicle weaver. Lastly, a boy with a connection to both shadow and light."

Understanding the gravity of Umbralis's request, Eldarion nodded solemnly. Umbralis, without hesitation, urged Eldarion to tap into his memories to witness the detailed plan. Eldarion, using his skill to connect with Umbralis's memories, saw the intricacies of the chosen warriors and the unfolding events.

"In eighteen years," Umbralis declared, his gaze unwavering, "I will be waiting in the Chronicle Chamber. With you as my witness, I will finally come clean to Elowen, and surely with you with as my witness he will believe me."

To solidify the trust between them, Eldarion proposed a pact. Umbralis, recognizing the sincerity behind Eldarion's intentions, readily agreed. Eldarion insisted that Umbralis always tell him the truth and seek help when needed.

Umbralis, ever the alchemist, devised a clever solution. He proposed using his alchemical skills to conjure a rune command that would mark them both. The mark's effect would be to incapacitate anyone who lied, rendering them powerless and forcing them to speak the truth.

Eldarion, amused by Umbralis's ingenuity, couldn't help but shake his head in admiration. The plan, though unconventional, provided a sense of reassurance. As the rune command was set, Umbralis couldn't suppress a chuckle, foreseeing potential fortune in his future endeavors.

With Umbralis restored to his true self and a plan set in motion, the two friends shared a moment of relief. Eldarion, ready to play his part in the unfolding destiny, acknowledged the complexities that lay ahead. The enchanted chamber, privy to their pact, echoed with a sense of anticipation as the secrets of Eldermere continued to unravel.

Eldarion, now connected telepathically with Umbralis, relayed his arrival and sought guidance for the next steps. Umbralis signaled Eldarion to bring the three individuals into the chamber. Without hesitation, Master Elowen, Kaelin, Lirael, Eldarion, and their familiars entered the chamber. The entrance sealed behind them, enveloped in shadows

As they walked towards the light at the end of the room, a figure sat above, shrouded in mystery. Suddenly, the person leaped down, landing gracefully, and began walking toward the group. Master Elowen, Kaelin, Lirael, and their familiars, on high alert, readied their weapons, and prepared for any threat.

Eldarion calmly walked past the trio, standing beside the unknown person. The sudden shock and confusion gripped Master Elowen and the others, prompting a barrage of questions. With weapons at the ready, Elowen was about to unleash a concentrated beam when the voice spoke, halting his actions.

"You don't recognize me, Elowen?" said the mysterious figure. Elowen, still guarded, replied, "Should I know you?" Slowly, as the hood covering the figure's face was pulled back, realization dawned on Elowen, and a mix of emotions played across his face.

The figure revealed his face, and it was none other than Umbralis. Shock and astonishment echoed among the trio. Eldarion, standing by Umbralis's side, wore a knowing smile, having played his part as a witness to this long-awaited reunion.

*"I've done my part, Umbralis. Now, everything is up to your plan,"* Eldarion had telepathically communicated to Umbralis earlier, and the pieces of the puzzle were finally falling into place.

Umbralis, now free from the dark entity's influence, stood before his old mentor and comrades, ready to reveal the truth behind the recent events. The enchanted chamber, witness too many revelations, held its breath as Umbralis began to recount the tale of the dark entity, the split artifact, and his journey to break free. The threads of destiny continued to weave, connecting the past to the present in the heart of Eldermere's mystical chamber.

As Kaelin and Lirael exchanged puzzled glances, their confusion palpable in the air, Master Elowen's keen gaze fell upon them. Sensing their uncertainty, he took a step forward, a knowing smile playing at the corners of his lips.

"Allow me to introduce you to someone who may shed some light on the mysteries that surround us," Master Elowen said, his voice steady and reassuring. With a graceful gesture, he beckoned forth the enigmatic figure who stood at the edge of the chamber, veiled in shadows.

"Kaelin, Lirael, meet Umbralis," Master Elowen announced, his voice tinged with reverence. "He is also a part of the Luminary Consortium just like I was in the past.

"Umbralis, a luminary from the Consortium?" Kaelin's eyebrows shot up in surprise. "I thought the Consortium no longer existed.

Master Elowen exchanged a knowing glance with Umbralis before addressing Kaelin's question. "The Luminary Consortium, while diminished, still exists in the shadows, Kaelin. Its influence may not be as overt as it once was, but its legacy endures, woven into the very fabric of Luminary itself."

Umbralis nodded in agreement. "Indeed, Kaelin. The Consortium's presence may be subtle, but its purpose remains steadfast—to safeguard the balance of magic and knowledge in our realm."

Kaelin furrowed his brow, processing this newfound information. "But why remain hidden? Why not emerge to confront the threats that plague Luminary?"

Umbralis offered a cryptic smile. "Sometimes, Kaelin, the truest power lies in the shadows, guiding events from afar. The Consortium's wisdom is timeless, and its influence extends beyond the realms of light and darkness."

With those words lingering in the air, Kaelin's mind buzzed with newfound understanding, and the trio prepared to delve deeper into the mysteries that awaited them, guided by the enigmatic presence of Umbralis and the legacy of the Luminary Consortium.Top of Form

Master Elowen nodded solemnly. "Indeed, Kaelin. While the Luminary Consortium is renowned for its luminaries of Aether and elemental magic,

Umbralis represents a different facet of our organization—a guardian of the shadows, if you will."

"Umbralis has quite the intriguing backstory," Master Elowen remarked, his eyes sparkling with pride. "Unlike Eldarion and I, who were born and raised here in Luminara, Umbralis arrived as an alchemist I invited to join our ranks. Under the formality of the organization, he became my apprentice."

Umbralis nodded a hint of nostalgia in his gaze. "Indeed, those early years were a time of discovery and growth. It wasn't long before I stumbled upon a new application of shadow magic—a breakthrough that caught the attention of the Luminary Consortium."

Master Elowen beamed with admiration. "Umbralis's dedication and ingenuity proved him to be more than just an apprentice. Within three years, he had ascended to become one of the Luminary Consortium's esteemed members, a testament to his skill and determination.".

Master Elowen turned to Umbralis, his eyes gleaming with curiosity. "Umbralis, there are so many questions I've been meaning to ask you," he began, his voice filled with anticipation. he added, "Where were you when all of the other members gathered in the meeting hall on the day of the invasion from the Void Shaper?"

Umbralis, now standing before his old friend and comrade, spoke with sincerity, "Elowen, Kaelin, Lirael, and dear friends, I know you have many questions and I owe you an explanation. The events that transpired were beyond my control, but now, I am free, and the truth must be revealed."

The enchanted chamber, which witness too many revelations, held its breath as Umbralis began to recount the tale of the dark entity, the split artifact, and his journey to free himself from its influence. The trio, along with their familiars, lowered their weapons, listening intently to Umbralis's story, while Eldarion stood by, his role as a witness fulfilled. The threads of destiny continued to weave, connecting the past to the present in the heart of Eldermere's mystical chamber.

Elowen, Lirael, and Kaelin stood in amazement as Eldarion took charge, expressing his desire for the truth to be unveiled through his advanced chronicle-weaving skill. Eldarion, confident in his abilities, requested assistance from his familiar, Atticus, to conjure a field connected to the elements and another layer that would amplify his Chronicle weaving skill. The goal was to transport Elowen, Lirael, and Kaelin back to witness pivotal moments in the past.

Umbralis, recognizing the necessity of revealing the truth to Eldarion, trusted him and his unique skills. Eldarion, with a mischievous grin, playfully demanded his reward from Umbralis.

"Umbralis, you owe me big time for this," Eldarion teased. "I want a foot massage and one of your delicious meals after this, you hear me?"

Umbralis, in a subtle act of evasion, purposefully looked away and hesitated before finally responding, "I can make you all the food you want after this, Eldarion. And once again, thank you for the help."

With the agreement settled, Atticus conjured the instructed field, and Eldarion began casting his combined skill with Atticus—Chronicle Weaving - Time of the Essence. The magical field expanded into the air, transporting them to a place resembling the past.

Eldarion, taking on the role of a guide, explained, "What you see here is the truth and nothing but the truth." Elowen and his apprentices observed how Umbralis had been used to perform the circle and unleash Master Voss. They witnessed Umbralis fighting for his life, seeking Eldarion's help, and discovered the connection between the reason Kaelin and Lirael were left in the care of Master Elowen.

The scenes unfolded before them like chapters of a forgotten book, revealing the intricate web of events that had shaped the present. As the visions of the past played out, the truth became clearer, and the mysteries that had haunted Eldermere began to unravel. The enchanted chamber, resonating with the echoes of the past, bore witness to the unfolding revelations that would reshape the fate of Eldermere.

"Within the enchanted chamber, as the Chronicle Weaving - Time of the Essence unfolded the past, a cascade of colors swirled around them, carrying the echoes of history. The air buzzed with magic, and each character's heartbeat synchronized with the revelations.

Elowen's eyes widened, a mix of shock and recognition playing across his face. Lirael and Kaelin exchanged glances, their expressions shifting from confusion to understanding. Umbralis, standing resolute, bore the weight of his past decisions.

Amidst the unfolding scenes, the unknown woman's presence became more pronounced. Her gestures, words, and the determined glint in her eyes painted a portrait of someone deeply committed to a cause. She wasn't merely an ally; she was a key player in the grand tapestry of destiny.

As the vision continued, the realization dawned on Lirael and Kaelin. Their parents' decision to entrust them to Master Elowen wasn't a mere whim; it was part of a meticulous plan crafted by those who sought to safeguard them. The enchanted chamber resonated with the gasps of realization and the soft rustling of memories falling into place.

Amid this revelation, a subtle foreshadowing emerged. The vision hinted at the birth of Aric, a figure intricately woven into the fabric of Eldermere's destiny. Umbralis and the mysterious woman, glimpsed in the past, held the key to a saga yet to unfold.

As the last echoes of the vision faded, the characters stood in the enchanted chamber, their minds filled with newfound understanding and the promise of a destiny yet to be unraveled."

"There is someone I want you all to meet" said Umbralis. His's gaze shifted purposefully, his hand gesturing towards Erebus, his enigmatic companion. With a whispered incantation, Erebus conjured a shimmering portal, its surface rippling with otherworldly energy.

As the portal stabilized, a figure materialized within its depths, emerging from the ethereal mist with an aura of quiet strength. The enchanted chamber pulsed with anticipation as Umbralis, through the mystical portal conjured by Erebus, heralded the return of Kaelin's parents, Elyndor and Avonlea, and Lirael's parents, Zephyria the Galewhisperer and Ignatius, The Emberforge Warden. The air crackled with energy as the familiar faces materialized, their expressions a mix of determination and accomplishment.

The large screenslike portal came alive, not with mere images, but with the living presence of these dedicated individuals who had ventured into the realms of ancient knowledge and mysterious landscapes. Their narratives echoed through the chamber, recounting the challenges they faced in pursuit of the relic fragments and information. Each word painted a vivid picture, immersing the onlookers in the rich tapestry of their quests.

The chamber, once still, now vibrated with the collective resolve of the group. The shared experiences and insights forged a deeper connection among them, a unity born from the trials faced by their predecessors. As the tales unfolded, the participants felt a profound sense of purpose, understanding the gravity of the impending confrontation with the encroaching shadows.

Amid this shared knowledge, Umbralis, with a measured intensity, unveiled another vital chapter. Through the portal, Erebus brought forth Umbralis's wife, Luminos - The Prismancer. Her arrival bathed the chamber in a radiant glow, her mastery over light and energy evident in every movement. The group, now complete with the reunited families and Umbralis's wife, stood united in the face of the approaching shadows.

# CHAPTER 32

# EMBRACE OF LUMARIAN LEGACIES

The enchanted chamber, a silent witness to the ongoing saga, stood as a testament to the enduring bonds forged in the crucible of darkness. The stage was now set for the next chapter, with the united group prepared to confront the shadows that loomed ominously ahead.

As the portal conjured by Erebus hummed with ethereal energy, a surge of anticipation filled the chamber. The air crackled with a mix of magical resonance and the collective determination of those present. Slowly, figures emerged from the portal, stepping into the enchanted chamber with a blend of familiarity and awe.

Kaelin's parents, Elyndor and Avonlea, materialized with a stoic resolve etched on their faces. Their eyes, filled with the wisdom of countless adventures, met the gaze of their son. Lirael's parents, Zephyria and Ignatius, followed suit, their presence commanding the attention of those around them.

Umbralis, a mixture of relief and satisfaction evident in his eyes, greeted them. "Welcome back, dear friends. Your dedication and sacrifices have paved the way for the next chapter in our quest to safeguard Eldermere."

The group, now complete with the arrival of Kaelin and Lirael's parents, exchanged glances, a silent understanding passing among them. The resonance of familial connections and shared purpose lingered in the air, strengthening their resolve.

Amidst this reunion, Umbralis turned towards the radiant figure beside him. "Allow me to introduce my wife, Luminos - The Prismancer," he declared, his voice carrying the weight of both reverence and love. Luminos, with a graceful bow, acknowledged the assembly. Her presence, a beacon of light in the mystical chamber, added a new dimension to the unfolding events.

Eldarion, perceptive as ever, felt the intricate threads of destiny weaving a tapestry of interconnected lives. "Our journey is far from over," he remarked, his eyes reflecting the glow of the chamber. "With each ally, each revelation, we inch closer to unraveling the mysteries that shroud Eldermere."

The group, united by a shared past and a destiny yet to unfold, stood in the enchanted chamber, ready to face the challenges that awaited them. The Chronicles pulsated with the energy of past, present, and the promises of the future, echoing the resilience of those who dared to defy the shadows.

Overwhelmed by a mix of emotions, Kaelin and Lirael felt a surge of relief seeing their parents step through the portal unscathed. The weight of uncertainty lifted from their hearts as the truth unfolded before them — their parents were not lost or gone but actively involved in a quest to protect Eldermere.

Without hesitation, Kaelin rushed towards his parents, Elyndor and Avonlea, tears welling up in his eyes. Lirael, equally moved, ran towards Zephyria, and Ignatius. The enchanted chamber became a witness to a heartfelt reunion as the children embraced their parents, a connection forged through love and an unbreakable bond.

Elyndor placed a reassuring hand on Kaelin's shoulder, a silent acknowledgment of the trials they had faced. Avonlea gently brushed away a tear from Kaelin's cheek, her eyes reflecting a mix of maternal warmth and pride.

Zephyria held Lirael close, her comforting presence a source of solace for her daughter. Ignatius, his stern exterior softened by the genuine affection for his child, whispered words of reassurance to Lirael.

The chamber, filled with the soft glow of magical energies, became a sanctuary for this poignant moment of family reconnection. Eldarion, Umbralis, and Luminos observed the touching scene, recognizing the significance of this reunion in the grand tapestry of their shared destiny.

As the embrace lingered, a sense of unity and purpose resonated within the group. The trials they faced and the challenges ahead seemed surmountable with the strength drawn from familial ties and the bonds they had forged. The Chronicles whispered tales of resilience and love, etching another chapter in the mystical history of Eldermere.

## Lirael's POV:

Zephyria, holding Lirael in a tender embrace, spoke with a voice as gentle as a breeze. "My dear Lirael, I want you to know that your father and I have always been watching you, even if from a distance. We may not have been there in person, but we were there in spirit, witnessing every step of your journey."

She paused, looking into Lirael's eyes with an expression of both apology and love. "I apologize for not being there to witness your growth personally, to share in your joys and guide you through challenges. However, connected to the wind as I am, I've been a silent companion, guiding you in ways that might not always be apparent."

Zephyria's words carried the weight of a mother's regret and the warmth of unwavering support. "The wind has whispered your name, and I have listened. I've seen the strength within you, the resilience that has blossomed over the past sixteen years. You've grown into a remarkable individual, and I couldn't be prouder."

Lirael, though moved, felt a comforting reassurance in her mother's words. The revelation of her parents' constant presence, even from afar, added a new layer to the tapestry of her life. The enchanted chamber, filled with familial love and magical energies, became a sacred space for healing and understanding.

Ignatius, with his characteristic stern demeanor softened by the warmth of the moment, stepped forward to stand beside Zephyria and Lirael. His eyes, usually firm and serious, now held a gentleness that spoke volumes.

"Lirael," he began, his voice deep yet filled with sincerity, "I may not express myself as openly as the wind but know that every blaze in my forge, every flicker of flame, carried a silent prayer for your well-being. I've watched you navigate the winds of life with resilience and grace, just like your mother."

He placed a calloused hand on Lirael's shoulder, a gesture both paternal and reassuring. "I may not have been physically present, but my spirit has been with you every step of the way. Trust in the strength you've cultivated, and remember, the ember of my guidance will always burn bright within you."

Lirael, feeling the genuine love and guidance from both her parents, nodded with a mixture of gratitude and understanding. The reunion in the enchanted chamber became a poignant moment of connection, healing the wounds of separation and reaffirming the unbreakable bonds of family

As Ignatius spoke and the words resonated in the chamber, Lirael's eyes widened with realization. The mysterious guidance she had sensed throughout her magical journey, the subtle nudges that steered her through adventures, and the comforting presence during moments of uncertainty— all fell into place.

A gentle smile graced Lirael's lips as the pieces of the puzzle clicked together. "It was you, guiding me all along, wasn't it?" she whispered, looking at both Zephyria and Ignatius.

Zephyria, nodded with a tender expression. "The winds carried not only whispers of the world but also the echoes of our guidance. You were never alone, my dear Lirael. The elements conspired to watch over you and nurture the magic within."

The enchanted chamber, witness to revelations and reunions, held an atmosphere of profound connection. Lirael, now understanding the source of the guidance that had shaped her magical journey, felt a renewed sense of purpose and gratitude. The bonds with her parents, strengthened by the shared acknowledgment of their presence in her life, created a moment that transcended time and space.

Earlier this year as the celebration of Lirael's sixteenth birthday unfolded, Master Elowen, with a knowing twinkle in his eyes, presented her with a set of special gifts. Alongside the usual birthday cake and presents, he brought forth a sealed letter, an intricately crafted staff, and a delicate locket containing a picture. The items were entrusted to him by Lirael's parents, Zephyria the Galewhisperer, and Ignatius, The Emberforge Warden.

Elowen, aware of the significance of these gifts, had patiently waited for the right moment to reveal their purpose. Now, with the events in the enchanted chamber connecting the past and present, the mystery behind these items began to unfold.

"Lirael," Elowen spoke, his voice carrying a blend of warmth and solemnity, "these gifts are not just tokens of love from your parents. They are symbols of guidance, strength, and a connection that surpasses time itself."

As Lirael opened the sealed letter, the words within carried the essence of Zephyria and Ignatius's guidance, expressing their love and the hope that, on her sixteenth birthday, she would come to understand the significance of the gifts.

The intricately crafted staff, when held by Lirael, resonated with magical energy, a conduit to the elements and a testament to her lineage. The picture locket, when opened, revealed the smiling faces of Zephyria and Ignatius, frozen in a moment that transcended the years they had spent apart.

In that enchanted moment, Lirael felt a profound connection to her parents, as if their love and guidance were present in the very air around her. The chamber, witness to the unfolding of destinies, held the echo of a celebration that spanned both time and realms.

Kaelin's POV

Kaelin, overcome with a torrent of emotions, approached the shimmering portal conjured by Erebus. The enchanted chamber hummed with magical energies as Umbralis, understanding the gravity of the moment, offered a comforting smile.

"Kaelin," Umbralis spoke, his voice a blend of warmth and wisdom, "your journey has been one of resilience and discovery. But there's more to unravel, and your parents have played a crucial role in this intricate tapestry."

Kaelin, wide-eyed and overwhelmed, took tentative steps toward his parents. Elyndor, usually composed and dignified, struggled to contain the welling emotions. Avonlea, radiating a motherly warmth with water-themed sparkles, opened her arms in a heartfelt invitation.

"Kaelin," Elyndor's voice carried both pride and emotion, "we've watched you grow from afar, every step filling our hearts with pride. The path you've walked, though challenging, has shaped you into a remarkable young man."

Avonlea, tears of joy shimmering like droplets, added, "You were always in our thoughts, our silent encouragements carried by the winds. Now that we stand here together, the separation feels like a distant dream."

Kaelin, embraced by his parents, felt a flood of emotions. The support he had felt throughout his life, the silent encouragement during moments of uncertainty—all found their origin in the unwavering love of Elyndor and Avonlea.

Umbralis, with a knowing smile, gestured toward the enchanted chamber. "The threads of fate weave a complex tale, and now, with your parents by your side, a new chapter begins. Together, you'll discover the significance of your role in the destiny that awaits."

The enchanted chamber, witness to the reunion of families and the interplay of destinies, held an atmosphere charged with emotion and anticipation. Kaelin, surrounded by the love of his parents, prepared to uncover the truths that awaited him in this mystical realm.

As Elyndor and Ignatius approached Elowen and Eldarion, a subtle shift occurred. Elyndor, feeling a sense of relief, allowed a glimpse of his chaotic characteristic nature to emerge. A mischievous glint danced in his eyes as he exchanged a knowing look with Elowen, their shared history allowing for a more open expression of their true selves. Ignatius, usually stern and reserved, found himself becoming more talkative in the presence of his old friend.

Meanwhile, at the back of the enchanted chamber, Avonlea, Zephyria, and Luminos shared warm embraces, overjoyed by their long-awaited reunion. The three women, connected by the threads of destiny, exchanged greetings and laughter.

Observing their husbands' interaction, Avonlea couldn't help but let out a sigh. "I guess some things will never change," she remarked.

Zephyria nodded in agreement. "Indeed, Avonlea. Men will be men—they are just kids in grown-up bodies."

Luminos, with a serene smile, joined the conversation. "I apologize that Umbralis dragged you all, and your families, into this," she said, acknowledging the complexity of the situation.

Avonlea reassured her, "No need for apologies. We are all connected by fate, and facing challenges together only strengthens our bonds. We'll get through this, as we always have."

The group, now reunited, shared a moment of camaraderie amidst the magical ambiance of the chamber. The echoes of laughter and shared stories wove a tapestry of connections, demonstrating the resilience of friendships that transcended time and circumstance.

Umbralis, sensing the need to refocus on the task at hand, subtly signaled Luminos to stand by his side. The group, understanding the shift in the atmosphere, gathered in a large circle at the center of the enchanted chamber and sat down at a big round table. The echoes of laughter and reunions now gave way to a more serious tone as Umbralis prepared to initiate the next phase of their plan.

With everyone assembled, Umbralis took a moment to address the group. "Thank you all for being here and for your unwavering support. Our reunion is a testament to the strength of our bonds, but we must now turn our attention to the imminent threat—the dark entity that lurks in the shadows."

The atmosphere in the chamber grew solemn as Umbralis continued, "We are gathered here not just as friends and allies but as the chosen defenders of Eldermere. The relics we seek, and the destinies we carry, all lead to this moment. Our actions will determine the fate of this realm and beyond."

Umbralis glanced at each member of the group, his gaze holding a mixture of determination and trust. "Luminos, if you may," he gestured, allowing his wife to contribute to the unfolding plan.

Luminos stepped forward, her radiant presence illuminating the chamber. "The key to sealing the dark entity lies not only in the relics but also in the unity of our strengths. Each of you possesses unique abilities, and together, we can forge a barrier that will confine the dark entity and prevent its malevolent influence from spreading."

As Luminos spoke, a soft glow emanated from her, symbolizing the harmonizing of their powers. The group, now standing in a circle, understood the gravity of the situation. Each member felt the weight of their destinies intertwining, bound by a shared purpose.

Umbralis, with a determined look, concluded, "Let this enchanted chamber bear witness to our resolve. Together, we shall face the darkness that threatens Eldermere. Now, let the preparations begin."

The group, fueled by a sense of unity and purpose, started the preparations for the intricate ritual that would harness their collective strengths to seal the dark entity. The chamber, witness to the ebb and flow of destiny, awaited the unfolding of the final confrontation between light and shadow.

Umbralis and Luminos, standing side by side, continued their discussion, casting a focused gaze upon the group. It was time to unveil the final piece of the puzzle—the identity of a crucial figure in their plan, a boy named Aric.

Umbralis shifted his focus, his gaze holding a certain intensity. "Now, there's another key player in this intricate dance," he continued, "Aric, a skilled individual, is diligently working on a mission to keep a close eye on Master Voss. His unique abilities are vital to our plan, adding an extra layer of protection against the looming threat we face."

The others exchanged glances, a silent acknowledgment of the importance of this mysterious figure. Luminos, with a knowing smile, chimed in, "We've entrusted Aric with a critical role, and his efforts are essential in countering Master Voss's moves." The air in the enchanted chamber buzzed with anticipation, the final piece of the puzzle still veiled in a shroud of secrecy.

A sense of curiosity and confusion rippled through the group. Before they could inquire further, Luminos, with a warm smile, interjected, "Oh, we forgot to mention, didn't we? Silly of us. Aric is our child."

The revelation hung in the air, and the group processed the information, realizing the intricate family ties that bound Umbralis, Luminos, and Aric. The enchanted chamber, witness to numerous revelations, echoed with a sense of unity and determination as the group prepared for the final stages of their plan.

# CHAPTER 33

# HARMONY UNRAVELED: CONFRONTING UMBRAXIS AND GAIASURGE

Umbralis, standing at the heart of the enchanted chamber, extended a hand to gather everyone's attention. In the roundtable, their expressions were a mix of anticipation and concern. Before they could delve into Elyndor's team report, Elyndor and Avonlea stood up and stepped forward, ready to share their findings.

Elyndor, the embodiment of pure aether energies, and Avonlea, with water-themed sparkles surrounding her, began detailing their exploration of Eldermere. Their report painted a vivid picture of the dark entity's pervasive influence, detailing the corruption that seeped into the once-pristine landscapes.

"As we ventured into the heart of Eldermere," Elyndor began, his voice carrying the weight of the aetheric energies he wielded, "the very essence of this realm seemed to rebel against its natural order. The ley lines, once conduits of harmonious energy, now resonate with dissonance. The corruption is deep-rooted, and its source is unlike anything we've encountered before."

Avonlea added, her eyes reflecting the deep connection to the water element, "The rivers and lakes have become tainted, mirroring the turmoil within Eldermere. Elemental creatures are twisted into dark aberrations, and the very air is heavy with the scent of corruption."

The group listened intently, absorbing the gravity of the situation. The unfolding narrative emphasized the urgent need to counteract the dark entity's influence.

Elyndor continued, "As we followed the corrupted ley lines, we encountered runes strategically placed across key locations. These runes amplify the dark entity's power, serving as anchors to its malevolent influence. The culprits behind this strategic deployment are two members of the Decagon Shadow Court—Umbraxis, the Void Commander, and Luxara, the Luminous Shade."

Umbraxis and Luxara, the mysterious generals of the Decagon Shadow Court, were introduced as architects of the runic corruption. Umbraxis, with mastery over the void and shadow, and Luxara, a blend of light and shadow, had been diligently spreading these runes across Eldermere, tightening the dark entity's grip.

Umbralis, listening with a grave expression, nodded in understanding. "Umbraxis and Luxara are formidable adversaries. Their collaboration signifies a union of opposing forces, a delicate balance between light and shadow that we must unravel."

Eldarion, attuned to the elements, spoke up, "To counteract these runes, we'll need to disrupt their connection with the corrupted ley lines. Luxara's affinity with light might be our key to finding the ley line disruptions."

Umbralis, acknowledging the insights, turned to Luminos. "Luminos, with your ability to manipulate light, you may be able to detect the disruptions Eldarion mentions. Together, we can strategize a plan to dismantle these runes and weaken Umbraxis and Luxara's hold on Eldermere."

The group, now armed with crucial information, shifted their focus to the upcoming mission. The enchanted chamber, witness to the unfolding saga, held the collective determination of those who dared to confront the shadows threatening their realm.

Umbralis, his gaze reflecting a blend of determination and concern, spoke, "Our quest becomes more perilous with each revelation, but together, we shall unravel the mysteries shrouding Eldermere and confront the Decagon Shadow Court. Let our unity be our strength in the face of this looming darkness."

Zephyria and Ignatius, having ventured to the west side of Eldermere, took their turn to report the unsettling encounters they faced. As they stepped forward in the enchanted chamber, the air seemed to carry a subtle weight, foreshadowing the gravity of their findings.

Zephyria, the Galewhisperer, began to recount their journey. "The western reaches of Eldermere are no less affected by the encroaching darkness," she spoke, her voice carrying the essence of the wind. "The once vibrant forests are now silent, and the winds whisper tales of imbalance in the elements."

Ignatius, the Emberforge Warden, continued, "As we delved deeper, we also encountered Umbraxis, the Void Commander, orchestrating the corruption. His mastery over the void proved to be a formidable challenge. The very earth beneath our feet trembled, resisting its corruption with defiant strength."

Their words hung in the air, and a sense of unease settled over the group. Umbraxis, the enigmatic Void Commander, seemed to be orchestrating the darkness with a meticulous hand.

Zephyria pressed on, "In our confrontation with Umbraxis, another figure emerged—Gaiasurge, the Elemental Eclipse. This entity wields power over Earth, Light, and Shadow, creating an intricate dance of opposing forces. The corrupted landscapes mirrored Gaiasurge's influence, a testament to the delicate balance these generals maintain."

Ignatius added, "Gaiasurge's ability to manipulate both light and shadow amplifies the corruptive forces. It's as if the very elements are at war within Eldermere, and Gaiasurge is the orchestrator of this chaotic symphony."

Umbralis, absorbing this new information, contemplated the intricate dynamics of the generals. "Umbraxis and Gaiasurge, working in tandem, present a formidable challenge. Their control over opposing elements suggests a level of coordination we have yet to fully comprehend."

Eldarion, with a thoughtful expression, spoke up, "Their connection to Earth, Light, and Shadow forms a triad of elemental forces. We must consider this balance in our approach. Disrupting one element might expose vulnerabilities in the others."

Umbralis, acknowledging the insight, turned to Luminos. "Luminos, with your understanding of light, you may hold the key to unraveling the complexities of Gaiasurge's manipulation. Together, we can exploit the delicate balance these generals maintain."

## Veilwalker's Revelation: The Unseen Threads of Destiny:

The group, now armed with the knowledge of Umbraxis and Gaiasurge's influence, began strategizing. The enchanted chamber, witness to the unfolding revelations, echoed with the determination of those who stood against the impending darkness.

Umbralis, addressing the group, said, "The challenges ahead are immense, but with each piece of information, we gain clarity. Zephyria, Ignatius, your insights are invaluable. Let us weave a plan that disrupts the delicate balance Umbraxis and Gaiasurge maintain."

As the group prepared for the next phase of their mission, the enchanted chamber pulsated with a mixture of anticipation and resolve. The fate of Eldermere hung in the balance, and the allies, bound by destiny, steeled themselves for the confrontations that lay ahead.

Upon receiving reports from Zephyria and Ignatius, Umbralis's heart sank as he realized the dire nature of the situation. "This is bad," he muttered to himself, his mind racing with the implications of Aric's continued captivity within the void Sectum. It dawned on him that Master Voss likely saw Aric as a crucial vessel, explaining the shadow general's interference with the ley lines of Eldermere. Gathering his resolve, Umbralis knew he had to share his concerns with the rest of the group. "Before we proceed," he began, his voice tinged with urgency, "there's something you all need to know. Luminos and I... we sent our son, Aric, and now we must retrieve him."

As Umbralis conveyed his concerns to the group, a solemn hush fell over the enchanted chamber. The revelation that Umbralis and Luminos had sent their son, Aric, weighed heavily on the hearts of all present. It added a layer of complexity to an already perilous situation.

Zephyria and Ignatius exchanged glances, understanding the depth of Umbralis's worry. They knew that retrieving Aric from the clutches of the void Sectum was now not just a mission to save a valuable ally but also a deeply personal quest for Umbralis and Luminos.

With a nod of understanding, Zephyria spoke up, her voice steady despite the gravity of the situation. "We stand with you, Umbralis. Saving Aric is not just a matter of duty but one of familial love and loyalty. We will do whatever it takes to bring him back safely."

Ignatius, his expression grave, added his agreement. "Indeed, we cannot allow Master Voss's machinations to tear apart families and manipulate destinies for his ends. Aric must be rescued, and the ley lines of Eldermere must be protected."

Elowen, his concern evident in his eyes, questioned Umbralis about the decision to send Aric into the void. "So why did you send him into the void in the first place? Isn't it safer if he was with me, like Kaelin and Lirael?" Elowen added, seeking an explanation for the risky choice.

Umbralis, his gaze reflecting a mix of regret and determination, responded to Elowen's inquiry. "Luminos and I agreed that to truly understand the void itself, one must be deeply connected to it. Our purpose for letting Aric be taken by Master Voss was to harness his unique power against him. We believed that Aric's connection to the void could be a formidable weapon in our hands."

He continued, his voice carrying the weight of regret. "However, after careful consideration, I realize that I have truly risked my own child's safety. Evangeline is a genius, and even now, I am connected to her fortunately they are in a cavern resting and waiting for the my next command. She plays a crucial role in ensuring Aric's well-being and disrupting the ritual that threatens Eldermere."

Umbralis's admission hung in the air, the complexity of the situation unfolding before the concerned allies. The enchanted chamber, witness to the revelations and discussions, resonated with a somber acknowledgment of the sacrifices made in the pursuit of safeguarding Eldermere.

Elowen, though understanding the strategic reasoning, couldn't entirely mask his worry. "Risking a child, even for such a noble cause, is a heavy burden. We must act swiftly and decisively to rectify this situation and ensure Aric's safety," Elowen asserted his commitment to protecting the young boy unwavering.

Umbralis nodded, acknowledging the gravity of the situation. "Our focus now is to disrupt the ritual and prevent Master Voss from recapturing Aric, severing Master Voss's connection to the void, and bringing Aric safely back to Eldermere. Together, we shall face the challenges that lie ahead and safeguard the realm from the looming shadows."

As the communication between Umbralis and Evangeline unfolded, the mystical connection between the two realms intensified. The enchanted chamber, a silent observer of the unfolding events, resonated with the heightened magical energies.

Suddenly Evangeline's voice is connected to Umbralis, carrying a tone of urgency and dedication, echoed through the connection. "*Master Umbralis, Aric's connection to the void has evolved. He has become a VoidWalker—a being with the ability to traverse between worlds and connect directly with the void's essence. This transformation grants him unique insights and capabilities that we can leverage in our fight against Master Voss.*"

Umbralis, though relieved by the potential advantages of Aric's newfound abilities, couldn't shake off the concern for his son's emotional state. "*Aric is resting right now, but I am afraid he is confused and angered about what happened*" added Evengeline. "*Evangeline, his confusion and anger are understandable. This transformation must be overwhelming for him. We need to guide him through this, help him comprehend his role, and ensure he remains anchored to Eldermere.*"Evangeline, always composed and analytical, responded with a sense of reassurance. "*I am by his side, Master Umbralis. I will do everything in my power to guide him through this tumultuous experience. The connection between Aric and the void is strong, and I believe we can utilize it strategically. However, we must address his emotional state to fully harness his potential.*"

Umbralis nodded in acknowledgment, appreciating Evangeline's dedication to both Aric and the greater cause. "*Keep me updated on his condition, Evangeline. We must work together to bring him back safely and use his abilities to counteract Master Voss's plans.*"

The communication channel crackled to life as Evangeline's voice reached Umbralis in the enchanted chamber. The revelation about the Umbral Arbiter Veilwalker and Aric's connection to both shadow and light hung in the air, casting a profound impact on the gathered allies.

Umbralis, his brow furrowed in contemplation, urged Evangeline to share more details. *"Tell me, Evangeline, what did this Umbral Arbiter reveal about Aric's connection to the light? How does it intertwine with his link to the shadows?"*

Evangeline, her tone reflective, began to elucidate the intricate details. *"Master, the Umbral Arbiter spoke of Aric as a VoidWalker—a being capable of traversing the void and attuned not only to shadows but also to the celestial light. It seems that Aric's unique heritage, a convergence of shadow and light, grants him a profound connection to both primal forces."*

Umbralis, absorbing the information, considered the implications. The cosmic balance, already teetering on the edge, now faced an unprecedented twist with Aric's role as a VoidWalker. The shadows and light interwoven within him held the potential to shape the destiny of Luminary in unforeseen ways.

Evangeline continued, *"The Arbiter hinted at an ancient prophecy, a choice that Luminary must face. Aric's connection to the light adds a layer of complexity to this cosmic event. The shadows and light converge in him, making him a pivotal figure in the impending celestial alignment."*

Umbralis, recognizing the significance of Aric's dual nature, shared the revelation with the assembled allies in the enchanted chamber.

The air crackled with a sense of urgency as the group grappled with the intricate threads of destiny woven around Aric. *"Luminary stands at a crossroads,"* Umbralis addressed the allies. *"The Umbral Arbiter suggests that Aric's unique connection to both shadow and light is entwined with an ancient prophecy. Our choices and actions in the coming events will shape the destiny of realms beyond."*

As the allies absorbed the weight of Aric's dual nature and the impending cosmic event, the enchanted chamber became a crucible of strategizing and contemplation. The Umbral Arbiter Veilwalker's cryptic guidance hinted at a cosmic dance that would unfold with Luminary standing at the epicenter—a dance that would shape the destinies of shadow and light.

As the Umbral Arbiter Veilwalker's enigmatic words echoed through the Voidshaper Sanctum, Evangeline's alchemic senses heightened, absorbing the gravity of the cosmic forces at play. The revelation that Aric, connected not only to the void but also to the light, unveiled a layer of complexity in the unfolding cosmic drama.

Evangeline, with a mix of curiosity and concern, pressed the Umbral Arbiter for more information. *"What do you mean, connected to the light? How does Aric's link to both shadow and light affect the balance you seek to maintain?"*

The Umbral Arbiter, its form shifting like ephemeral shadows, responded with deliberate ambiguity. *"Aric embodies a convergence—an intersection of primal shadows and celestial light. This duality is rare and holds the potential to tip the cosmic balance in unforeseen ways. Luminary's destiny, intricately woven with threads of both shadow and light, is now poised at the brink of a profound choice."*

Evangeline, absorbing the weight of the cosmic revelation, pondered the implications. The shadows whispered secrets that hinted at an ancient *prophecy*, a choice that would define the fate of Luminary. The Umbral Arbiter, as the Veilwalker, was here to guide the realm through the impending celestial alignment and the choice that accompanied it.

*"The celestial alignment is not merely a convergence of stars; it is a cosmic event tied to Luminary's pivotal moment,"* the Umbral Arbiter explained. *"As Aric grapples with the duality within him, Luminary teeters on the edge of a choice that will shape the destiny of realms beyond. The shadows weave a tale of uncertainty, and only the cosmic dance will reveal the path that awaits."*

Evangeline, realizing the magnitude of the revelation, conveyed the information to Umbralis and the gathered allies in the enchanted chamber. The cosmic forces at play, the impending celestial alignment, and Aric's role as a conduit between shadow and light added layers of complexity to their mission.

As the communication channel closed, the allies in the enchanted chamber exchanged glances, understanding the gravity of Aric's transformation. The concept of a VoidWalker, a being with a direct link to the void's essence, added a new dimension to their strategy against the dark entity.

Umbralis, deep in thought, considered the implications of Aric's abilities. The pieces of the puzzle were falling into place, and he realized that Aric's unique connection to the void could be a game-changer in their confrontation with Master Voss.

"His transformation into a VoidWalker may just be the key we need," Umbralis mused aloud. "With Aric's ability to connect directly to the world, we can gain valuable insights and perhaps uncover vulnerabilities in Master Voss's plan. We must tread carefully, but this might be the turning point we've been seeking."

The group, fueled by a renewed sense of hope, prepared for the next phase of their mission. The enchanted chamber, still resonating with the echoes of the communication, held the promise of strategic revelations and the potential to shift the balance in their favor in the looming battle against the shadows.

As the celestial alignment drew nearer, the Veilwalker's presence lingered in the shadows, a silent guardian navigating the cosmic currents. Luminary, standing at the crossroads of destiny, awaited the moment when the veil would be lifted, and the threads of fate would be unveiled in the cosmic tapestry that bound them all. The enchantment of the chamber resonated with a sense of anticipation, echoing the cosmic symphony that played out in the celestial realms.

Umbralis's wife, her eyes reflecting a mix of concern and understanding, approached him in the enchanted chamber. She gently placed a hand on his shoulder, offering a reassuring smile. "Umbralis, our son is resilient. He carries within him the strength of both shadow and light. Evangeline is with him, and together, they will navigate through this transformative journey. Have faith in Aric's innate abilities and the bonds that tie him to Eldermere."

Umbralis, appreciating the comforting words of his wife, nodded with a mixture of gratitude and determination. The weight of responsibility still pressed upon him, but her reassurance provided a momentary respite. "Thank you, my love. We must press on with our mission, ensuring that Aric's sacrifice and transformation lead to the safeguarding of Eldermere."

As the couple shared a brief moment of connection amidst the unfolding events, the enchanted chamber stood witness to the familial bonds that strengthened their resolve. The echoes of reassurance lingered in the air, becoming a source of strength for Umbralis as he prepared to face the challenges ahead.

# CHAPTER 34

# VOIDBOUND RESURGENCE

Umbralis, driven by a paternal concern, connected telepathically to Evangeline and requested, *"Evangeline, connect me to Aric. I need to speak with him."*

Evangeline, acknowledging Umbralis's request, focused her magical abilities on establishing a connection between Umbralis and Aric. The mystical energies in the enchanted chamber resonated as the communication channel with the void opened once more.

Umbralis's voice, filled with a mix of worry and fatherly affection, reached out to Aric, *"Aric, my son, how are you holding up? I understand this must be overwhelming, but your connection to the void is crucial. We need your insights to counteract Master Voss's plans. Remember, you are not alone, and we are here to guide you through this."*

Aric's response carried through the void's mystical connection and conveyed a mixture of confusion, anger, and a faint glimmer of realization. The father and son, separated by the ethereal boundaries between realms, shared a moment of connection in the cosmic dance of light and shadow.

Aric's voice, tinged with fear and uncertainty, resonated through the void. *"Pa, I... I don't understand what's happening. The void, the shadows—it's all so overwhelming. I feel lost."*

Umbralis, his paternal instincts taking precedence over the dire situation, responded with soothing reassurance. *"Aric, my son, I know this is a challenging moment. The void can be perplexing, but remember, you are strong, and you're not alone. We're connected, and together, we'll navigate through this. Trust in your abilities, and trust in us."*

Evangeline, attuned to the emotional currents in the void, added her supportive words, *"Aric, you hold a unique power within you. Embrace the connection to the void, let it guide you. Your father and I are here for you every step of the way. You're not alone in this journey."*

The enchanted chamber, a silent witness to the emotional exchange, resonated with the comforting words that traversed the void. Amid the uncertainty, the bond between father, son, and mentor became a beacon of support—a light cutting through the shadows that threatened to engulf Aric.

Umbralis, hearing the mix of emotions in Aric's voice, felt a pang of guilt and understanding. *"Aric, my son, I know you're feeling a whirlwind of emotions, and I apologize for the choices we've made. But Evengeline's right— we must focus on the task at hand. Your strength and resolve are admirable."*

Evangeline, sensing the need for connection and support, reassured Aric, *"Aric, your evolution into a VoidWalker was not a mistake. It has granted you abilities that can help us in this fight. We're here to guide you and support you. Let the void be your ally, not a source of fear."*

Aric, determined to contribute despite his inner turmoil, spoke with a newfound resolve. *"I'm mad at you, Pa and Ma, but we can address that later. Right now, I want to be useful. I need to play my role. Guide me, Pa, and connect me with Ma. I don't want to stay weak. It was Master Voss's mistake teaching me and evolving me into a Voidwalker, but I want to play my part. You owe me big time, Pa, and I want your chicken sandwich."*

Umbralis, recognizing Aric's resilience, responded with a mix of pride and understanding. *"Aric, your determination is commendable. We will guide you through this, and together, we'll navigate the challenges that lie ahead. And don't worry, when you return, you'll have the best chicken sandwich Eldermere has ever seen."*

The enchanted chamber, still resonating with the intertwined threads of emotion and determination, became a focal point for the allies. The impending confrontation with Master Voss loomed, but the bond between father, son, and mentor remained unbroken—a source of strength in the face of adversity.

Luminos, feeling the connection with her son Aric, responded with a mix of emotions. *"Aric, my dear, it's not about thinking you're fragile. I worry because you're precious to me. But I see the strength in you, the courage that has grown. We believe in you, and I'm here to support you every step of the way.*"

Aric, determined to reassure his mother, spoke with a newfound confidence. "*Ma, don't worry about me. I'm not that cowardly, fragile boy I used to be. I've evolved, and I'll make sure that strength counts in the battles to come. Your guidance has shaped me, and I'll do my best to make you proud.*"

Luminos, touched by Aric's words, conveyed her pride and love. "*Aric, you've grown into a remarkable young man. Remember, strength is not just physical; it's in your heart and spirit. Face the challenges with the wisdom you've gained. I'll be right here, connected to you, offering my guidance and love.*"

The communication channel between mother and son held a sense of warmth and determination. The enchanted chamber, witness to this familial exchange, resonated with the intertwining threads of love, strength, and the unyielding bond between the members of Luminary.

Aric, now connected with both Umbralis and Luminara, nodded with determination. "*Right now, we need to focus on bringing you back home, Aric,*" Umbralis affirmed, his voice carrying a mixture of reassurance and urgency. "*We have a plan to disrupt the ritual and sever Master Voss's connection to the void. Evangeline and the rest of us will work together to ensure your safe return.*"

Luminos, her motherly concern evident, added, "*Your safety is our priority, Aric. We'll guide you through this process, and once the ritual is disrupted, we'll bring you back to Eldermere. Your strength and our unity will see us through this challenge.*"

Aric, resolute in his decision to play an active role, responded, "*I'm ready, Pa, Ma. Guide me through this, and let's make sure Master Voss regrets underestimating the power of Luminary.*"

The enchanted chamber, charged with the collective determination of Umbralis, Luminara, and Aric, held the promise of a united front against the encroaching shadows. The allies, bound by familial and mystical bonds, prepared to face the challenges that awaited them in the void realm.

The allies, witnessing Aric's determination and resolve, rallied around the shared goal of bringing him back from the void. Eldarion, Zephyria, Ignatius, Elyndor, Avonlea, and the others expressed their willingness to offer their assistance in disrupting the ritual and ensuring Aric's safe return.

Evangeline, the alchemic enchantress, reminded Umbralis of his familiar's presence. "*Master Umbralis, don't forget that your familiar, the shadowy companion, is with us. Its connection to you might be instrumental in navigating the void realm and facilitating Aric's return. Together, with our combined efforts, we can turn the tide against Master Voss.*"

Umbralis, acknowledging the support and considering Evangeline's insight, focused on the unity forged among the allies. "Thank you, everyone, for your unwavering commitment. Let us harness the strengths of each member and work in harmony to rescue Aric and thwart Master Voss's plans."

The enchanted chamber, resonating with the collective determination of the gathering, became a focal point for strategizing and channeling their combined magical energies. The next steps in their mission were crucial, and the allies prepared to venture into the void realm united, each contributing their unique abilities to ensure Aric's safe return.

Aric, fueled by determination and a newfound sense of purpose, looked to Umbralis for guidance. Evangeline, with a reassuring nod, extended her hand, summoning Umbralis's familiar—a mystical creature bound to Umbralis's magical essence. The familiar, an ethereal creature resembling a shadowy raven, materialized in the Void, its eyes glowing with a soft, comforting light.

Umbralis, his voice carrying the weight of paternal concern, spoke, "*Aric, focus on the familiar. It is an extension of my magical essence, a bridge that connects us across the realms. Let its presence guide you, and allow it to become the conduit through which we communicate.*"

Aric, his gaze fixed on the mystical raven, concentrated on forming a connection. Evangeline, channeling her alchemic powers, wove a supportive enchantment, enhancing the familiar's ability to serve as a stable link between Aric and the realm of Eldermere.

As the connection strengthened, Umbralis's voice resonated through the link, *"You are not alone, Aric. The familiar will guide you back to Eldermere. Let its essence surround you, and trust in the connection we share."*

Evangeline, her alchemic aura intertwining with the familiar's energy, added, "You possess incredible strength, Aric. Embrace the Voidwalker within you, and let the familiar be your guide. We are here to support you every step of the way."

The enchanted chamber, a silent witness to this interdimensional communication, vibrated with the harmonious convergence of magic. The other members of the gathering extended their supportive energies, creating a collective force to aid Aric's return from the Void.

Aric, drawing upon his newfound abilities, allowed the familiar's essence to envelop him and Evangeline. The Void, once a daunting expanse, now felt less foreboding as the mystical raven guided them through the shadows and cosmic energies that intertwined in the space between realms.

Umbralis, Luminos, and Evangeline maintained the connection, their combined efforts ensuring Aric's safe traversal through the Void. The familiar, acting as a beacon, led Aric toward the threshold that separated the realms.

As the transition between realms neared completion, Aric's and Evangeline's silhouette materialized in the enchanted chamber. The gathering, witnessing his return, felt a collective exhale of relief. Aric, though wearied by his journey through the Void, stood with newfound resolve, his connection to the realm and its guardians stronger than ever.

Umbralis, overcome with paternal relief, approached Aric and placed a reassuring hand on his shoulder. "Welcome back, my son," Umbralis uttered, a mix of pride and concern in his eyes. "Your strength and resilience have proven invaluable."

Aric, meeting Umbralis's gaze, nodded with a hint of a smile. "I may be mad at you, Pa, but I'm ready to play my part. No more being a fragile boy. And, by the way, you owe me that chicken sandwich."

The enchanted chamber echoed with a shared moment of levity, a respite amid looming shadows. The group, united by the successful return of Aric, now turned their attention to the next phase of their mission—the confrontation with the Decagon Shadow Court and the unraveling cosmic forces that dictated the fate of Eldermere.

# CHAPTER 35

# VEILWALKER'S REVELATION

The return of Aric to the enchanted chamber brought a renewed sense of determination among the gathered allies. As they prepared for the challenges that lay ahead, the mystical ambiance of the chamber became a focal point for strategizing and sharing the revelations from the Void.

Umbralis, his gaze fixed on Aric, spoke with a mix of paternal concern and pride, "Aric, you've shown remarkable strength. Your connection to the Voidwalker within you will be a crucial asset in our upcoming endeavors. Now, let us delve into the knowledge you gained during your time in the Void."

Aric, still adjusting to the transition, recounted his experiences. "The Void is both chaotic and serene. It's a place where shadows dance with cosmic energies and the boundaries between reality and unreality blur. In that realm, I sensed a presence—the Umbral Arbiter Veilwalker."

The mention of the Umbral Arbiter drew the attention of the gathered allies. Eldarion, attuned to cosmic energies, spoke, "The Umbral Arbiter is a cosmic guardian, an entity born from the convergence of primal shadows and cosmic energies. What insights did this Veilwalker offer, Aric?"

Aric continued, "The Umbral Arbiter revealed that I am not only connected to the Void but also to the celestial light. I am a Voidwalker entwined with both shadow and light. This connection, according to the Arbiter, holds the key to Luminary's destiny and an ancient *prophecy*."

Umbralis, absorbing this revelation, exchanged a knowing look with Luminos. "The cosmic balance teeters on the convergence of shadow and light. Aric's dual nature makes him a pivotal figure in Luminary's fate. What does the Umbral Arbiter suggest about the impending celestial alignment?"

Aric, delving into the Arbiter's cryptic guidance, shared, "The Arbiter hinted at an ancient choice that Luminary must face. The shadows whisper of a force beyond Master Voss and even Umbraxis—the cosmic dance of destiny awaits, and our decisions will shape the ultimate fate of our realm."

Evangeline, her alchemic senses heightened, added, "The Umbral Arbiter is not bound by allegiance to light or shadow. It seeks to maintain cosmic balance. Our path forward is intertwined with this cosmic dance, and Luminary stands at the crossroads of a profound choice."

Umbralis, considering the intricate threads of fate, addressed the allies, "The Umbral Arbiter's guidance aligns with our mission. Aric's connection to both shadow and light makes him a key player in the cosmic events unfolding. We must decipher the ancient *prophecy* and make choices that safeguard the balance."

As the allies absorbed the revelations, the enchanted chamber resonated with a sense of cosmic significance. The Umbral Arbiter's presence hinted at in Aric's journey, added a layer of complexity to their mission. The allies, bound by destiny, stood ready to unravel the cosmic threads that wove the tapestry of Luminary's fate.

The chapter concluded with the allies forming a plan, their minds focused on the celestial alignment and the choices that would define the realm's future. As they ventured deeper into the heart of Eldermere, the shadows of the impending cosmic dance cast both uncertainty and determination over their path.

Umbralis, his gaze thoughtful, addressed the gathered allies in the enchanted chamber. "Before we embark on our paths, there are crucial matters that demand our attention. Let us convene and share our insights on countering the threats posed by Umbraxis, Luxara, and Master Voss. The convergence of elements and shadows requires a united strategy."

Eldarion, attuned to the cosmic energies, spoke with a sense of urgency. "The delicate balance between light and shadow must be maintained. As we explore the runes and uncover the mysteries of Eldermere, we must remain vigilant. The cosmic dance is intricate, and any disruption may tip the scales in unforeseen ways."

Zephyria, the Galewhisperer, added her perspective. "In the west, Ignatius and I witnessed the orchestrated chaos created by Umbraxis and

Gaiasurge. Their control over opposing elements is formidable. Disrupting their coordination is paramount, and understanding the elemental balance they maintain is key."

Ignatius, the Emberforge Warden, nodded in agreement. "Gaiasurge's manipulation of Earth, Light, and Shadow poses a unique challenge. We must strategize to exploit the vulnerabilities within this triad. Each element, intricately connected, can be a source of both strength and weakness."

Luminos, the Illuminarch, interjected, "As we confront these challenges, let us not forget the cosmic guidance provided by the Umbral Arbiter Veilwalker. The celestial alignment approaches, and the destiny of Luminary is entwined with cosmic threads. The arbiter's enigmatic insights may hold the key to our success."

Umbralis acknowledged their perspective's and proposed a plan. "Our unity is our strength. Let us synchronize our efforts, combining the wisdom of runes, the mastery over elements, and the cosmic insights. Avonlea's knowledge of runes will be invaluable, and with the understanding of the elemental balance, we can form a comprehensive strategy."

The seasoned allies, united in purpose, engaged in a collaborative discussion, sharing their expertise and formulating a plan that would address the challenges posed by Umbraxis, Luxara, and Master Voss. The enchanted chamber, witness to their strategic deliberations, echoed with the resonance of their determined resolve.

As their discussions reached a consensus, the seasoned members prepared to share the formulated plan with the younger members, ensuring that every ally, regardless of age or experience, played a crucial role in the unfolding cosmic saga of Eldermere. The next chapter awaited, promising a convergence of knowledge, power, and destiny.

Elowen, his concern evident in his eyes, addressed Umbralis with a pressing matter. "Umbralis, we can't face these challenges alone. The other members of the Luminary Consortium need to be brought up to date on the unfolding events. Their knowledge and abilities are crucial in this cosmic struggle."

Umbralis nodded in agreement, recognizing the importance of unity within the Luminary Consortium. "You're right, Elowen. Our strength lies in our collective wisdom and power. We must gather the others and share the insights we've gained. Each member's unique abilities contribute to our overall strategy."

Elowen, determined to ensure the Consortium's cohesion, took charge. "I'll reach out to the other members, update them on the situation, and bring them here. We need everyone aligned in our purpose to safeguard Eldermere."

Umbralis, appreciating Elowen's initiative, added, and "Coordinate with them, Elowen. Share the details of our discussions and the plan we've formulated. Their contributions are invaluable, and together, we shall face the challenges that lie ahead."

As Elowen prepared to contact the other members of the Luminary Consortium, the enchanted chamber resonated with a sense of shared responsibility. The unity of the Consortium, a beacon of hope in the face of encroaching shadows, would play a pivotal role in the cosmic dance that awaited them.

The next chapter would unfold with the convergence of the Luminary Consortium, each member bringing their unique strengths to the forefront, forging a bond that transcended individual abilities—a bond forged in the crucible of shared destiny.

Avonlea's words resonated in the enchanted chamber, her water-themed sparkles shimmering with a sense of purpose. The allies turned their attention to the water elemental as she expressed her insights regarding runes and hinted at a place of significance.

With a determined gaze, Avonlea continued, "Runic knowledge is not only powerful but deeply interconnected with the essence of Eldermere. There's a place, a sanctum hidden within the heart of the realm, where the ancient wisdom of runes is preserved. To access it, I must attune myself to the water currents and decipher the ethereal patterns."

Umbralis, recognizing the potential significance of this revelation, nodded in approval. "Take the time you need, Avonlea. The wisdom of runes may hold the key to countering Umbraxis and Luxara's influence. In the meantime, let us ensure that our younger members understand the importance of their roles in this cosmic struggle."

Eldarion, ever attuned to the cosmic energies, addressed the younger members of the gathering. "Kaelin, Lirael, and the talented Aric, there is much to learn about the intricate dance of runes I'm sorry to say this but the three of you need to gain runic magic and Avonlea here is a master of said branch of magic. Therefore I suggest that Avonlea guide you through the ancient knowledge that intertwines with the elements. Your understanding of runes will be a valuable asset in the battles to come we want you to be ready for the challenge to come."

Avonlea, with a gentle smile, spoke directly to the three younger members, "Hey, lovelies!" Avonlea's voice was filled with excitement as she addressed the younger members. "How about we swing by to my hometown, Atlanta, and explore some rune magic together? It's gonna be so much fun, and you'll feel the elemental vibes of Eldermere. I promise you, it's gonna be an absolute blast!"

The group dispersed, the seasoned members preparing for their respective tasks while Avonlea took the younger ones under her wing. The enchanted chamber, witness to the unfolding destinies, echoed with a sense of anticipation as the allies embraced their roles in the cosmic dance that would determine the fate of Luminary. The next chapter beckoned, promising revelations, challenges, and convergence of mystical energies that would shape the destiny of Eldermere.

To Be Continue ...